MALCOLM
under the
STARS

MALCOLM
under the
STARS

BY
W. H. BECK

PICTURES BY
BRIAN LIES

HOUGHTON MIFFLIN HARCOURT

BOSTON   NEW YORK

The text of this book is set in 11.45-pt. Palatino LT Standard.

The illustrations are pencil and powdered graphite on vellum.

Library of Congress Cataloging-in-Publication Data

Beck, W. H., 1970–

Malcolm under the stars / by W. H. Beck ; [illustrated by Brian Lies].

p. cm.

Summary: When a rare coin and a strange code are uncovered in
McKenna School, Malcolm and the other classroom pets of the Midnight
Academy take on their most challenging assignment yet and, through
their investigations, they just might save the school from closing.

ISBN 978-0-544-39267-0

[1. Mystery and detective stories. 2. Rats as pets—Fiction.

3. Pets—Fiction. 4. Animals—Fiction. 5. Coins—Fiction.

6. Ciphers—Fiction. 7. Schools—Fiction. 8. Secret societies—Fiction.

9. Humorous stories.] I. Lies, Brian, illustrator. II. Title.

PZ7.B3812Mar 2015

[Fic]—dc23

2014037484

Manufactured in the United States of America

DOC 10 9 8 7 6 5 4 3 2 1

44500538031

FOR MY READER NIECES: ADA, ALEXANDRA,
ANNABELLE, EMILY, AND PAYTON
—W.H.B.

TO MY FRIEND MARK JUSTICE
—B.L.

Dear Readers,

One day last summer, I was working in my classroom when Ms. Brumble delivered my mail: a big manila envelope, thick with paper.

It was the following note and story.

I don't have any proof of who mailed it, but after reading, I think I Know (with a capital *K*). Maybe you will too.

I can't wait to share it with next year's fifth-graders.

Enjoy,

Mr. Mark Binney, fifth grade teacher

Dear Mr. Binney,

    We know. You didn't expect to hear from us again this year! But sometimes things don't happen as planned. (And some-times they do.) Anyway, we thought we owed you an explanation about why the newspaper and news stations called the school that morning. As you often say, there's usually more to the story.

    And, as Amelia likes to say . . . commas matter.

    Sincerely,

    Your Fifth Grade All-Stars

CHAPTER I
A SNEEZE

It began with a sneeze. Malcolm didn't mean to sneeze, but when you're a small rat stuffed into a fifth-grader's jeans pocket, these things happen. Especially if the pocket is, for some unknown reason, filled with pencil shavings.

Skylar, the owner of the pocket, jiggled at the sneeze, and Malcolm scrambled to stay upright. Crumb! This was no good. Back in Room 11, when Skylar had held out his hand, Malcolm had jumped at the chance to go with him to the class's rehearsal of the fifth grade program.[1] After all, Malcolm had never been to McKenna Elementary

---

[1] "America the Beautiful: A Musical Road Trip Across Our Great States."

School's auditorium before, and it was his duty—as a member of the school's secret society of classroom pets, Midnight Academy—to seize these opportunities when they presented themselves. Besides, Skylar carried Cheezy Bits Snack Crackers in his pocket. It is hard for anyone to think around Cheezy Bits Snack Crackers.

But so far this afternoon, all Malcolm had seen was the inside of Skylar's pocket. The *other* one. The one filled with pencil shavings. Malcolm was beginning to think Amelia had been right to shake her head at Skylar's invitation.

Nevertheless, he was here, so he might as well use his eyes, ears, nose, and whiskers to report something back to the Midnight Academy. He fought his way up to the edge of the pocket and stuck his nose out. Ah—already this was better: fresh air.

He scanned the view. Skylar and the rest of the fifth-graders (or "nutters," as the Midnight Academy liked to call kids; "lankies" were grownups) swayed to the refrain of "Rocky Top." Kiera, decked out in pink sequins, warbled in the spotlight with a much-coveted solo.

Mrs. Findlay paused her piano playing, and the song creaked to a halt. "Kiera, this is not *American Idol*. Please, just sing. No need to stalk about the stage." The rest of the students—including the two classes waiting in the audience—twittered. Mrs. Findlay wasn't done, though. She snapped her fingers at the back row on the risers. "You—singers in the back. You've got to stand still. The audience can see every little move." She turned and shaded her eyes. "Isn't that right, Mr. Binney?"

You sat up from your seat in the front row, Mr. Binney, and frowned. "Yes. What's going on back there? Skylar, do you need to use the restroom?"

Skylar wiggled his jeans around his hips, knocking Malcolm back down into the pencil shavings. "Um, what?"

The classes in the audience snickered again.

Tianna, Kiera's best friend, who happened to be standing next to Skylar on the stage, elbowed him. "Stand still!" she muttered under her breath. "You're making us look bad."

Jovahn leaned over from the other side of Skylar. "It's

3

only the fifth grade program, Tianna. Not *American Idol,* remember? And it's a rehearsal."

"It's Malcolm," Skylar said, pushing Malcolm down inside his pocket again. "He keeps poking his head out."

At the sound of Malcolm's name, another fifth-grader twisted around from the row in front of Skylar, her long black hair swinging back. "Is he okay? I told you not to bring him!" Amelia Vang whispered.

Jovahn held out his hand. "Dude, here. Give him to me."

Yes, this was a good idea. Jovahn Grayson probably also had strange things in his pockets, but he was definitely more predictable than Skylar. Malcolm crept out, climbing up to Skylar's shoulder. He was poised to make the leap to Jovahn, when, from high up above—a rustle. Then a low *thunk.* Malcolm's ears pricked up, and he tilted his head. In the rafters, a shadow shifted. A small shower of dust sprinkled down, and Malcolm's nose twitched. Dirt?

And then, with another *thunk,* the lights winked out, and the auditorium was plunged into darkness.

The nutters—onstage and otherwise—shrieked and hooted. In the dark, someone knocked into Skylar, and Malcolm somersaulted off his shoulder. He landed, hunched, on the risers as they rumbled with the feet of thirty panicked fifth-graders. Shoelaces whizzed by Malcolm's whiskers, and he latched on. Better to be *on* than *under* this foot.

4

"FREEZE!" Your voice boomed through the darkness, Mr. Binney, and the foot under Malcolm came to a standstill. Malcolm peered in your direction and saw a flashlight beam bobbing in the audience. "Nobody move. The lights will come on again. They always do. It's not like this hasn't happened lately—so SETTLE DOWN."

And like you commanded it, the power clicked back on.

"See? There." Mrs. Findlay laughed nervously from the piano. "That won't happen during our program tonight, right, Mark?" she asked you. She turned to the class, clapping her hands for attention. "Now—again. From the top."

"Actually, Mrs. Findlay"—you were leaping up the stage steps two at a time—"I think that's enough for today. The bell's about to ring." You whispered to her, "Tonight will be better. I promise."

As the class thundered off the risers, Amelia looked around. "Where's Malcolm?" she called to Skylar. He patted his pockets, panic blooming on his face.

"Relax—I got him," Jovahn said, hopping on one foot so he could untangle Malcolm from his shoelaces on the other.

"Oh, good. I was afraid—"

A hand clamped down on Jovahn's shoulder. More specifically, your hand, Mr. Binney.

"That's not a certain rat from our classroom, is it, Jovahn?"

5

"Uh—well . . . "

Just then, Amelia bumped her way over. To anyone else, she looked to be on her way out the door, but in one smooth motion, she grabbed Malcolm, adjusted the hood on her sweatshirt, and tucked him safely there.

Jovahn grinned. He held out his empty hands. "Ah—no, in fact!"

You nodded. "I see." Then you raised your voice to your best stage level. "Well, I sure hope he gets back to his cage and doesn't find his way out for a long, LONG time."

Amelia flinched but kept moving.

Whew. For the first time since Skylar had scooped him out of the cage to go to the auditorium, Malcolm took a deep breath and relaxed. It wasn't simply that he was safe in Amelia's hood. It was more than that. It was *Amelia*. It might partly be the therapeutic qualities of her strawberry shampoo, but mostly Malcolm Knew—knew with a capital *K*—that if there was anywhere in the world that he belonged, it was with Amelia. He'd do anything for her, and she would do the same for him.

As the rest of the class bottlenecked at the side stage door, Ms. Brumble, the night custodian (and your fiancée, Mr. Binney), joined you. "Whoa," she said, trying to hide a smile.

"Laugh all you want," you answered, rubbing your hair until it stuck up in spikes. "We have a long way to go before this bunch is ready to leave McKenna for middle school."

Deep in Amelia's hood, Malcolm twitched. *Leave? Huh?* He pushed his nose out.

He watched then as you gestured toward the lights. "What's going on, anyway? Sound system blow a fuse?"

Ms. Brumble shook her head. "Unfortunately not. That would be easier to fix. No, this is something bigger. I wish we could figure out what's going on. We had to submit a report to the Building and Grounds department. It's going before the school board tonight."

At that, Malcolm remembered. The shadow! The dust falling down! He glanced up toward the back corner rafters where he had heard the rustle and the *thunk.*

Then the last bell rang. Amelia merged into the bustling after-school crowd, and Malcolm had to snuggle down into her hood out of sight. He pulled a whisker into his mouth and nibbled as he considered. *Had* that shadow really moved? It was almost as if something—someone . . . some *critter*—had been up there. A shiver rattled down Malcolm's spine, all the way to the tip of his tail. Like . . . a cat? Malcolm had only known one cat in his life, but when you're a small rat, one is more than you ever want to know.

But it couldn't have been her. That cat—Snip—was gone. It wouldn't be the first time Malcolm had imagined her. Her scratchy voice, overlong claws, and spider breath haunted even Malcolm's best dreams of peanut butter–dipped pretzels. No, it had to have been something else.

But if not her, then what? And did it matter?

Maybe he did have something to share with the Midnight Academy after all. Maybe before the meeting on Thursday, he could sniff around a little, find out more.

Because, really, you meant for him to stay in his cage during the *school day*, right, Mr. Binney?

CHAPTER 2
HERO BRAIN

"The problem with you, Malcolm," Jesse James said, stuffing a french fry into his extra-large hamster cheek, "is that you suffer from 'hero brain.'"

Hours later, long after the buzz of distant voices and the strains of music from the evening performance of the fifth grade program had died down, Malcolm and his two hamster friends, Jesse James and Billy the Kid, were winding down a Nosh and Fodder tour. While not sanctioned (or even remotely approved of) by the Midnight Academy, sneaking down to the garbage cans of McKenna's cafeteria had become a regular routine for the three rodents. Because, it turns out, nutters throw away a lot of food. And rats and hamsters are nocturnal—and always hungry. So that's many stomach-grumbling hours to fill with a lot of temptation nearby.

Malcolm had just finished telling his friends about the *thunk* and shadow in the auditorium. He leaned against the brick wall, stuffed. It had been a sloppy joe and baked beans day. "What do you mean?"

"'*Hero* brain'?" Billy repeated. "Are you sure you aren't suffering from 'french fry brain,' Jesse? Oof," she said, setting down a baby carrot in mid-nibble. "I can't eat another bite."

Malcolm made room for her next to him against the wall. They watched as Jesse mowed down another french fry like it was a pencil in a sharpener.[1]

"Yes," Jesse said around the fry, which extended his cheek to twice his width. "Hero brain. You know how last fall you saved all the nutters and the whole Academy from that crazy cat Snip, who wanted to poison the school? Everything worked out without a hitch. By crumb, you even got your lanky, Mr. Binney, and Ms. Brumble engaged and Honey Bunny — the grumpiest critter in the Academy — to be *nice*. So, after all that, now you feel like anything's possible. Your hero brain is all wired up, searching for some new quest to be conquered." He waved a french fry around like a sword. "But in reality, life's not like that. Life is mostly . . . well, let's put it this way: our most exciting

---

[1] Hamster cheek pouches go all the way back to their shoulders, and Jesse made good use of his on Nosh and Fodder nights.

days are sloppy joe/baked beans ones. Maybe walking taco day. Not a lot happens. What I'm saying is, chances are that was nothing up in those rafters. It was only your overactive hero brain."

His sister snorted. "So now you're calling Malcolm delusional?" She rolled her eyes.

"But what if it *was* something? Sometimes it is," Malcolm protested. "Don't we need to make sure?"

Jesse shook his head sorrowfully. He pointed the fry at Malcolm. "Hero-brain thinking again." He closed his eyes, hugged the fry to his chest, and said in a squeaky voice, "'If I just try hard enough, I WILL save the day.'" He opened his eyes and chomped the fry. "But really, it's about fifty-fifty. You got lucky with that cat last year, rat."

"So what's the point, then?" asked his sister. "According to you, there's no reason to ever try."

Jesse considered. He finished the fry and sat down next to them with a *thud*. His stomach bulged dangerously. "Well, I suppose that if you don't try at all, you don't even get a shot at that fifty percent."

Malcolm rolled to the floor and lay down on his back. He still wasn't sure he was following Jesse. But all that talk about Snip was making his stomach churn. "That's it, really," he confessed to the dark ceiling overhead. "What I'm scared of. For a bit this afternoon, I thought . . . it could have been . . . what if—"

"Spit it out," Billy said. "Well, not literally, please."

Malcolm sat up, took a deep breath, and blurted out the worry that had been worming around in his brain ever since the rehearsal that afternoon. "What if it was . . . a cat up there?"

Jesse slumped all the way to the floor and groaned. "Not again, Malcolm! Every time there's a wisp or a tap or a shadow or a breeze, you think it's a cat."

Malcolm rolled over. "I know."

Billy said softly, "She's gone, Malcolm. No one's seen her since you defeated her in the boiler room incident. The nutters, lankies, and critters no longer have to worry about her. Ever again. Thanks to you."

Gone. Because of him. Malcolm wasn't sure how he felt about that. In the end, he had felt . . . sorry for Snip. Yes, she was a deranged cat, but in a way, it wasn't her fault. She had only been wanting what the Academy critters had: Friends. Belonging. Safety. Love. She had just wished for them for so long and so hard that something in her had twisted, and the things she wanted the most became the things she hated the most.

Jesse sighed. "Come on." He struggled to his feet. He prodded Malcolm with his nose. Billy stood and stretched.

"What? Where are we going?"

Jesse was already moving across the cafeteria. He called over his shoulder, "To check out that shadow in the rafters. It was *not* Snip, but I know that hero brain of yours. You need to be sure it's not some other deadly threat to McKenna."

12

And Malcolm had to hide a grin as he trotted down the hall after the two hamsters.

It's good having friends who know you so well.

The auditorium's doors were shut tight, but that didn't stop a small rat and two escape-artist hamsters from finding a spot to squeeze through. Once inside, though, they all paused.

"Wow," Billy said. Malcolm agreed. Earlier, when he had been on the stage, it had been hard to see the enormity of the whole room with the bright lights shining on him. The room was huge! Vast,[2] even. Rows upon rows of velvety chairs, silent and folded. A little piece of him longed for a few minutes to go nuzzle that fabric—maybe after he checked the rafters.

"It was right about here," Malcolm said, climbing up the stage curtain above the far corner. Jesse plunked himself on the stage floor, claiming he was too full to climb. Billy crouched on a beam parallel to Malcolm, sniffing away.

A little moonlight shone in through the huge windows along the sides of the auditorium, but mostly Malcolm needed his nose and whiskers now, not his eyes.

"It was probably just dust falling down." Billy sneezed.

---

[2] Vast = huge, seemingly endless. Vocabulary from 2/11. What Kiera did not know about rats was vast.

"It's deep over here. I think this layer has been here since the school was built."

"Dusty and unused" was Malcolm's first analysis too. No critters had been up here in years. Could it have been simply dust knocked loose by the fifth-graders' activity? Maybe. But what was that *thunk*? Malcolm jumped over a coil of rope and followed a rafter to the wall, his paws padding softly. As he approached the outside wall, his nose twitched with a new scent. Wet wood.

He sniffed. There was a space here—a crack, really —just enough room in the crumbling plaster and worn wood for a small rat to squeeze into the side wall of the auditorium. Could another critter have done the same? A draft laced with cold and the definite scent of playground ruffled his whiskers slightly. Outside air? Crumb, that didn't seem right. "Hey," he called out to Billy. "I'm going to check something." He sucked in his stomach and squirmed in through the hole.

The stale air was thick inside the wall. Malcolm felt stringy lumps under his paws that must be wires. Gristle, Ms. Brumble should see these wires. They reminded him of untied shoelaces—limp and frayed. He followed them, the air getting colder and damper as he moved farther down the wall.

He reached a frame—a window or door of some sort —that butted against the bricks. His little rat map of the school in his brain clicked in, and he realized he was probably above the side entrance steps—the ones between the auditorium and the rest of the school. Malcolm pointed his nose straight up here, still following the scent of the outside. Near the top, the space widened, and Malcolm waded through piles of leaves, sticks, and fuzz.

Malcolm could make out the gray edges of the wall's supports now. As his eyes adjusted, he realized why: two of the outside bricks were askew on the outside wall. So crooked that the parking lot lights shone through the crack. Malcolm peered through the space between them. Just as he predicted, he was at the top of the wall, right under the eaves, where the auditorium addition joined the rest of the school building.

From here, he could see all the way across the parking lot to the oak trees, their trunks dark lines against the white of the snow.

A damp breeze rippled through his fur, his eyes watering from the cold. He pushed the leaves aside to get a better view through the cracks in the bricks.

And that's when something large (larger than Malcolm, anyway) and furry fell on Malcolm's head.

CHAPTER 3
SYLVIA

With a face full of fur (not his own), Malcolm plummeted down through the space between the inside and outside wall.

The two critters landed with a bump on the ground floor. Malcolm gasped for air as a bushy tail and the bottom attached to it landed on him.

He did the only thing he could think of to get a breath of air.

He nipped.

The furry bottom shot up, and Malcolm caught a foot in the eye.

"Ow!" Malcolm quickly backed away from the critter's sharp claws. He scrambled wildly through the loose leaves in the bottom of the wall.

"Look what you've done!" There was a little light here from the vent next to them in the wall. Malcolm saw that it was a gray squirrel chittering at him. (Malcolm did know what a squirrel was—he often watched them playing in the oak trees outside Room 11's windows.)

But before he could answer, Malcolm was pelted with three more critters.

"Whee!"

"Mama!"

"Mama!"

"My squirrelings!" The mother squirrel gathered her babies and curled her tail around them. They peered over it at Malcolm.

"What's that?" one asked, pointing his stubby tail.

"Can we do it again?" another asked. All three looked up at their mother.

"Certainly not." The squirrel drew herself up and stepped in front of the squirrelings to address Malcolm. "How dare you pull down our nest?" she scolded. "Where will we stay? It's not spring yet. Do you know nothing of the rodent rules?"

"I—" Malcolm started to say, then realized he really didn't know how to answer. Rodent rules? "I'm sorry. I didn't mean to pull down your nest. I was checking—"

She tapped her hind foot. "That's seven generations of nest you've managed to destroy in one minute."

"I didn't know . . . I . . ." Malcolm wondered whether Billy and Jesse could hear this conversation and if they'd come help him out. Maybe they knew the rodent rules? On second thought, they probably *could* hear and were laughing their whiskers off.

Malcolm straightened. Well, there was one thing he *did* know: his Midnight Academy training. Page seventeen of the handbook: "Always represent the Midnight Academy with dignity[1] and decorum."[2] Malcolm wasn't exactly sure what "decorum" meant, but he guessed it wasn't slinking away. And while this technically wasn't a Midnight Academy outing, the squirrel didn't know that.

"Ms. . . . Squirrel—" he started.

"It's Sylvia."

"Well, Sylvia—"

"And who are you? I didn't know there were rats in the neighborhood anymore."

"Yes, well, I'm Malcolm." Hold on. "You know I'm a rat?" Malcolm instinctively stood taller. He had grown a little in the last few months, but this was one of the very few times a species other than his own had recognized him.

"Are you mocking me?" Sylvia narrowed her eyes and tapped her hind leg again.

---

[1] Dignity = worthy of respect. Not a vocabulary word, but maybe it should be, Mr. Binney?

[2] Decorum = manners, basically. Vocabulary from 9/18. Mrs. Rivera insists on decorum in her office.

One of her squirrelings copied her. The other two stared. "Did he say he was a bat, Mama?"

Malcolm drew back. "What? A bat? No!" That was worse than being mistaken for a mouse!

He took a deep breath and began again. This time with

dignity. "Sylvia, I apologize about your nest. I was conducting official Midnight Academy business and did not know that it was there. May I offer to . . . make amends?"[3] This was the first time Malcolm had used one of Amelia's vocabulary words on his own out loud.

Sylvia's foot tapped faster. "Who?" she said. "What? I don't care. And I don't know about 'amends,' either, but if it means doing something about my nest, then fine. It may seem like spring's here, but there are a few cold snaps coming yet, and I don't want to be caught without a nest. I've got my squirrelings to think of, you know."

Malcolm's decorum wilted a little. "Of course," he said, lifting his right paw as one of the baby squirrels tried gnawing on it. He looked up at the dark expanse above them. "We could, well, maybe . . ." He gathered some of the fallen leaves and tried to climb back up.

The squirrelings giggled as Malcolm slid down in slow motion. "Going *up* with leaves never works," the smallest squirreling informed him. "You have to bring them *down*."

Sylvia leaned in to study Malcolm's face. "You're an Inside rat, aren't you?"

Malcolm wasn't sure what that meant. "Well, I live inside the building, yes. I'm a pet—"

"That explains it!" she said. "Inside critters don't know the first thing about survival." She poked Malcolm in the

---

[3] Amends = to fix a mistake. Vocabulary from 1/21. When Jovahn hurt Amelia's feelings by teasing a little too much about her color-coded notebooks, he made amends by buying her a matching pencil for each one.

chest with a claw. "Listen. It's not only the cold. I need a safe place for my squirrelings. They're not ready for the Outside yet. We don't have a cushy cage to protect us. There are Dangers in those trees: I can hear them, digging, moving around at night. It's why the Striped Shadow put us in this old nest when I asked him. And it's been perfect—until you stuck your nose in." She jabbed him again with a claw.

Cushy cage? "Look, I didn't even know you were in there—" Malcolm protested.

But Sylvia was already directing her squirrelings back up the wall. "The Inside rat is useless," she announced. "My darlings, we'll huddle until daybreak. Then I'll teach you how to rebuild."

Useless! Wait a minute. Malcolm raced after her. "I can help you. Just—"

She turned, tapping that foot again. Was that a small smile twitching her cheeks? "Well, I suppose I could teach you, too," she said slowly.

"Well, of course you can! I . . ." Malcolm paused. Aw, gristle. Had he been tricked? Sylvia was definitely grinning now. He sighed and held up a paw. "Wait here. I need to tell my friends I'm going to be a while. I'll be right back." He turned. Crumb, Jesse was never going to let him hear the end of this.

But before Malcolm could figure out how to explain what had happened, a bell rang out through the building. It went on and on, rattling Malcolm's teeth in his head.

Brrrriiiinnnnggg!

What the crumb? There was no Midnight Academy meeting tonight.

Malcolm hurried to the wall's opening. On the stage, Jesse flailed about, wild-eyed. The bell must have caught him in the midst of a post–Nosh and Fodder nap. "What's going on? Is it a fire alarm? Tornado drill?"

"No, cheddar brain. Wake up. It's a Tangerine Alert," said Billy, climbing down from the rafters. "Something's going on that can't wait until Thursday. We're supposed to report to the library within thirty minutes. I wonder what it is?" She bounced on her paws a little. "Let's go find out!"

"Yeah . . ." Malcolm looked over his shoulder toward Sylvia and the wall. Maybe if he worked fast he could still help rebuild *and* make the meeting. "Listen . . ."

"Did you find something?" Jesse asked in the middle of an enormous yawn.

"Not exactly," he started slowly. "But . . . I met someone. A family, really. Of squirrels. And the thing is . . . I kind of knocked down their nest. I think—" He looked back over his shoulder again. "I think they need my help rebuilding."

Jesse began to laugh. But Billy frowned. "There's a squirrel inside? That's not right."

Jesse poked her with a claw. "Now, now, haven't we learned that lesson already about who belongs and who doesn't?"

"I'm just saying, Outside and Inside critters don't mix.

23

It's a matter of survival. Outside critters don't understand our rules, and we don't know theirs. Critters don't last long on the wrong side."

This made Malcolm laugh. Was she kidding? "What? Rules? You've never followed a rule in your life, Billy! I'm pretty sure your whole Nosh and Fodder tours are not in that Academy handbook. And, besides, we're the Midnight Academy. Helping is what we do."

"We help the lankies and the nutters—Inside," she pointed out.

"But how do you decide who to help? And why?" This conversation made no sense to Malcolm.

Jesse finally stepped in. "What Billy's trying to say is that there are deeper rules—ways of life—than what's in the handbook. But it's fine." He held up a paw, and his sister stayed quiet. "You go ahead and fix their nest, hero brain. We'll let Aggy know you're on your way."

It took more than a few minutes, but in the end, Malcolm was able to help Sylvia rebuild her nest, despite being an Inside rat. He even impressed the squirrelings by successfully bringing *up* a few mouthfuls of leaves that were scattered all over the bottom of the wall. It seemed such a shame to waste them—they were already warm and dry. He tucked them around the squirrelings.

"Thank you, Malcolm," Sylvia said. "For an Inside rat, you make a pretty good nest."

"Thanks," Malcolm said. He had noticed that she had calmed down a little now that she knew her squirrelings were safe. He hesitated. He was still thinking of the shadow earlier in the day. "You know, sometimes there are Dangers Inside, too."

She nodded. "I suppose. But you have the choice about exposing yourself to them. We don't."

Malcolm thought about it. "Maybe. I guess." It sure didn't feel like it. Then he nodded toward the outside wall. "So . . . what kinds of Dangers are out there?"

She made a small whirring noise deep in her throat. "You have no idea." Then she laughed a little. "Actually, I don't either, really. I only know, as a rodent, I don't want to find out. It only takes one encounter with a Danger."

Malcolm nodded. That was the same instinct that made him stick to the shadowy edges of the hallways at night. "Well, if you ever hear of any, let me know. I thought I saw something earlier. It's why I was in the wall in the first place."

Sylvia smiled. "Will do, Malcolm. You can find us here until the snow melts."

"Thanks," Malcolm said again. And with that, he slipped down the wall and back out to the stage. He probably didn't have time to skirt the edges of the hall now, though. He was late for the Tangerine Alert.

CHAPTER 4
TANGERINE ALERT

Malcolm raced down the dark hallways to the library. How much time had passed? How late was he? As he approached the library, he heard other critters making their way to the meeting. Good––he wasn't the last one.

Thump. Thump. Thump.

Pitter-pat. Pitter-pat.

Scritch . . . scritch . . . scritch.

Malcolm followed, ducking under the door. A blue glow from a single computer on the front counter lit the room; Octavius the tarantula was already poised on its keyboard.

Malcolm raced up to the countertop and looked around, gasping for breath. "Aggy's not here yet?"

Pete the hermit crab shook his head.

"Neither is Polly or Tank," Billy pointed out.

"I'm telling you, there's going to be trouble," said Harriet, a hedgehog with more gray than brown in her whiskers. She stepped forward and sniffed. "That new initiative — allergy-free in the classrooms? — they're going to be going after us at McKenna next."

A huge white lop-eared rabbit hopped up. "Harriet, would you let it go?" Honey Bunny (or HB, as he strongly preferred to be called[1]) growled. He tossed his silky long rabbit ears. "We have enough in our food dish already. It's not that."

She coughed. "If you had to suffer allergies like I do, you wouldn't take this so lightly —"

Just then, Aggy Pop stormed into the library, her long green iguana tail swinging and her claws scritching on the floor. She held a rope clamped in her mouth, pulling a square scooter from the gym with Tank the turtle riding on it. She strode so fast, Tank swung wide and slammed into the doorjamb. Polly, a blue parakeet, followed, flapping hard to keep up with her.

Aggy didn't stop upon reaching the counter. In one fluid motion, she let go of the rope and climbed from the step stool to the chair onto the countertop. (Tank had it a little harder. Malcolm, Billy, and Jesse rushed down to push him up the two-by-four plank the Academy used for

---

[1] Yes, Honey Bunny's a he, despite the fluff-addled name the second-graders gave him. You should see his cage.

this purpose.) Polly came to rest on the computer monitor, almost as out of breath as Malcolm was.

"Thank you all for coming," Aggy said, nudging her head along the countertop, pushing a pair of red reading glasses[2] onto her nose. Her orange eyes loomed huge behind the lenses as she turned to the rest of the group. "I hope I wasn't interrupting your evening, but something has occurred that demands our immediate attention." She peered over her glasses at each critter in turn. "I don't mean to alarm you, but we are in the gravest of situations." She nodded up at the parakeet. "Polly?"

Polly let out a chirp, and her black and white wings fluttered. "Well, as you know, Tank and I video-conferenced with Van at the district Midnight Academy tonight."

Tank pushed his head out of his turtle shell. "There was a school board meeting. It got over a couple of hours ago. Well, when we heard, we told Aggy right away."

Pete scuttled forward, snapping his claw (the large one). "What happened?"

"I'm trying to tell you," Polly said. "If you'd quit interrupting me—"

But it wasn't Pete who interrupted next. It was a splash of water from the aquarium. "Oscar!" Billy said, and raced to the top of the tank behind Malcolm. "We always forget your light."

A giant orange and black fish swished by. He shoved his

---

mouth into the gravel and spit out colored beads. When he backed away, the gravel spelled out "I KNOW."

"Sorry," Malcolm said, and moved to the side so Oscar could see Polly.

"Honestly," Harriet scolded. "You think you two would remember. It's your one job—"

Aggy rapped her claws on the counter. Then she pulled them back. *Scriiiiitch.* "Really. We don't have time to squabble. This may be the most insurmountable problem McKenna has ever faced." She turned to Oscar. "I'm sorry, old friend. I should have thought of you."

The spines on Harriet's hedgehog forehead pricked up. She glanced between them. "What's going on? This isn't the allergy-free classroom initiative, is it?"

But the iguana simply nodded at Polly. "Please. Proceed."

"Okay. Um, so there was a school board meeting. And McKenna came up." She clacked her beak for a moment. "Tank, you're better at numbers."

"Somebody had better get telling," growled Honey Bunny under his breath.

Tank pushed himself to the center of the group. "The school board heard a report from the Building and Grounds department. About McKenna. It was twenty thousand dollars to replace the damaged windows in the upper floors this winter—the school board insisted on energy-efficient panes. And two hundred thousand dollars to fix the boiler room mishap last fall. The, uh, 'broken pipes' uncovered

a host of other problems with the plumbing." Malcolm winced as the Midnight Academy all looked his way. The pipes hadn't exactly been broken. He had gnawed through them. Granted, it was to stop Snip from putting her brew in the school's water, but, nevertheless, he had kind of . . . flooded the lower level of the school.[3]

Honey Bunny's whiskers twitched at Malcolm. "Hey, rat, it happens. The lankies don't always know how we help."

Malcolm ducked his head, and Tank continued: "And now this electrical issue. They're still trying to figure out what's going on. We've seen the wiring. We know that's not going to be good news."

"Well, it's a ninety-year-old school," Pete interjected. "What do they expect? Things get old, get worn out, maybe too small or outdated. You have to replace them. Upgrade." He tapped his claw on his shell. "I do it all the time."

Polly let out that funny little chirp again. "That's just it, Pete."

He raised his eye stalks to her. "What do you mean?"

Tank finished in a rush. "They're saying that the electrical system might not be up to code. If it isn't, they'll have to rewire the whole school, which will make the boiler room incident seem like loose change in the bottom of a backpack. The whole thing—well, it was proposed tonight that maybe McKenna's time has come."

---

[3] That's a whole 'nother story. A long one—a book, actually. Right, Mr. Binney?

For a moment, all anyone could hear was Harriet's allergic wheezing.

It was Malcolm who stepped forward. "What do you mean? 'McKenna's time has come'? Time for what? Repairs?"

Polly and Tank exchanged looks. "No, 'time' as in 'time's up.' They're talking about closing the school."

"What?" Jesse finally sat up.

"They can't do that!" Billy said. She looked ready to punch someone.

"Oh, but they've threatened that for y-years," Harriet sputtered. "They don't mean it."

Tank pulled his head into his shell. His voice was muffled from inside. "It's official now, though. The school board has scheduled two community 'listening sessions,' where lankies can say what they think of the idea. And then they'll vote."

A hush fell over the group.

Malcolm shook his head. He must have misunderstood this whole thing. Close the school? Was that even allowed? He walked around to look Aggy in the face. "Did they really say McKenna was going to *close?*"

Aggy slowly nodded.

Malcolm glanced around, a little wild-eyed. "But what will happen to the nutters if it closes? And the lankies? And what about us?"

Aggy said, "Well, if it comes to it, Malcolm, I imagine the nutters and lankies would go to a different school. And we'd stick with our lanky, most likely, and go to his or her new classroom."

Harriet tutted. "No, no, you're forgetting, Aggy. All the newer schools are pet-free. I've been trying to tell you."

"Oh, yes—how could we forget that?" Honey Bunny muttered.

"Gristle," Malcolm breathed. "So where *would* we go?" Malcolm literally couldn't picture it in his head. The only place he'd ever known was McKenna. McKenna and the Pet Emporium. And he couldn't go back there.

It was quiet for a moment. "We'd find homes, Malcolm," Aggy said. "A nutter family or your Mr. Binney would take you to live with them."

Harriet sighed. "I have a nutter—Tayler—who promises to take me home for the summer. He'd keep me, I know. Just think—one family. Quiet days. Sleeping in the sun instead of getting woken up by recorder practice." She looked around. "There are worse things than being sent to a nutter's home."

"Harriet!" Billy sounded appalled.

Malcolm didn't even know where to begin. What was "summer," for one thing? "How can you say that?! If we all get separated, there's no more Midnight Academy. And what would happen to the nutters and lankies without our help?"

Honey Bunny puffed out his chest. "But wait a minute. It's not closing for sure. They haven't decided anything. How much time do we have?"

"The first listening session is in three weeks in McKenna's auditorium," Polly answered.

"So . . . we figure out something! Come on—this is what the Academy is here for! What's our plan?" Honey Bunny hopped into the center of the group, his pink eyes darting from critter to critter.

There was a pause in the conversation then. Malcolm could hear Oscar's aquarium gurgling. But one by one, the critters blinked or looked away. Surely, there was something that could be done? Malcolm racked his ratty brain, but he didn't have any experience in anything like this. He was still a little unclear on who and what exactly a school board was.

"I don't suppose we critters can get up and speak at the listening session?" offered Billy.

"That would get them to close the school faster," muttered her brother. "I can see the headline: 'McKenna Overrun by Talking Vermin.'"

"Well, what's your idea?" Billy said, head-butting him.

Another pause. It was Harriet who spoke up. "I propose . . . we wait to see what the lankies' and nutters' action is first."

"What? You want to do nothing? You want to *wait?*" While Malcolm couldn't think of anything to suggest, this was, by far, worse than anything he was imagining.

Honey Bunny didn't seem to like it either. "Harriet, come on!"

The hedgehog's spines bristled. "I didn't say we

weren't going to do anything. But we don't want to run around like critters outside their cages for the first time. We need a plan. The lankies and nutters probably don't want the school to close either. Let's listen to their ideas tomorrow in our classrooms. Then we can know how to support them."

Harriet made sense. She did. But it didn't stop Malcolm from wanting to run around the library like a critter outside of his cage for the first time.

And that's when the group was interrupted by another splash from Oscar. They turned. Aggy was standing in front of the aquarium, blocking his message from view. "There is one idea," she said. "Oscar and I think it might be the only way to go. Or at least, it's worth thinking about." And she stepped aside.

Malcolm peered into the water at the new words in the gravel.

"THE LEGEND OF ERNIE BOWMAN."

CHAPTER 5

THE LEGEND OF ERNIE BOWMAN

"Ernie Bowman?" Malcolm said. "What's that?"

"Bowman? Like we should hire someone to tie the school board up in a bow?" Billy asked.

"No, no!" Jesse piped in. "It's a bowman. Like a bow and arrow. *Zing!*" He drew back and shot an imaginary arrow.

"Maybe it's the name of a good electrician?" his sister countered.

"This is no time for jokes!" Honey Bunny burst out.

Pete clicked his claws. "Do you two have oatmeal for brains?"

"It's just nervous energy," Billy explained. But she sat down.

"Well, what does Oscar mean, then?" asked Tank.

Harriet had been frowning this whole time. She cleared her throat. "It's a story. A . . . *legend,* as Oscar put it. But that's all it is." She turned to Aggy. "How can that possibly help with this?"

Aggy smiled slightly. (This did not make her look less scary, by the way. Have you ever seen an iguana smile?) "All legends are based on facts."

"Well, that's true." Polly tilted her head and considered. "We did just learn that John Henry might have been real."

"And Johnny Appleseed," mused Tank. "He was actually a man named John Chapman."

Malcolm didn't know any of these other people. And frankly, he didn't care. Not now, not with this news. "What is Ernie Bowman?" he nearly shouted.

Honey Bunny had been staring at Oscar's message, his pink nose twitching and his foot thumping. The sharp claws hidden in his silky fur made little tapping noises. He spoke slowly. "It's ridiculous, is what it is—" Honey Bunny started. Oscar aimed a wave of water at him. Honey Bunny ducked. "Watch the fur, fish!" He turned to Aggy. "You can't be thinking . . . This is what you've got? We're going to chase a fairy story to save the school? To save the Midnight Academy?"

Harriet turned to Malcolm. "It has to do with the beginning of the Midnight Academy. Didn't you learn this in your pledge training?"

"I, uh, didn't exactly have the regular pledge time," Malcolm reminded her, glancing at Honey Bunny, who shifted uncomfortably. The two critters had had a . . . misunderstanding when Malcolm had first come to McKenna. Malcolm had lied about who he was, and Honey Bunny had suspected that Malcolm was a skuzzy rat. But that's a different story. And discarded greens now, as Aggy liked to say.

"Oh, that's right. Well, this goes way, way back — before even the time of Thomas Jefferson, our founding guinea pig. Before McKenna was called 'McKenna.' It was Clearwater Central High School then, and it was beautiful. I've seen pictures." Harriet paused dreamily.

Honey Bunny sidled away from the aquarium and picked up the story. "Somewhere, or should I say some-*when*, back then, there was a man. We think. A teacher, maybe. Someone called Ernie Bowman. He always wore red suspenders."

"Suspenders?" Polly flapped her wings.

"Yeah, you know, those stretchy straps that lankies wear over their shoulders to hold up their pants? They're like a belt, but in the other direction."

Polly blinked. "What does that have to do with anything?"

"I don't know! It's just how the story goes!" Honey Bunny grumbled.

"Stories always have weird details like that," Billy offered.

"Anyway, the story *also* goes that he could . . . do stuff."

"He held the original Knacks," clarified Aggy.

Malcolm realized he was holding his breath. He let it out. "Wait—lankies can have Knacks?" He thought only critters had special skills and talents that the Academy called Knacks. Malcolm's was learning to read without actually learning to read. Octavius could type almost two hundred words per minute. Jesse and Billy prided themselves on being able to sneak into any room[1] undetected.

Aggy nodded. "Of course. Everyone—critter, lanky, nutter—has a Knack. The trick is recognizing and honoring them."

"Well, what were Ernie Bowman's?" Pete asked.

"It's said . . ." Honey Bunny shook his head. "This is crazy."

"Most stories are," urged Aggy. "The good ones, anyway."

Honey Bunny took a deep breath. "Fine," he said. "It's said that Ernie Bowman had powerful Knacks. He could grant wishes to nutters. He could turn dogs into silver."

"Why would you want to turn dogs into silver?" Pete asked.

"How should I know?" Honey Bunny glanced at Aggy, and only the force of her look kept him going.

Polly had been bobbing her head from her perch. "Wait . . . wait . . . I think I know this story." She jabbed her wing

---

[1] A secondary one that Aggy probably didn't know about was that Jesse could stuff seven french fries in his mouth at once. Billy was training to beat that.

out. "Could he bring a bird back to life with the touch of his finger?"

Honey Bunny nodded. "That's another one."

"Fried niblets, now *that's* a good Knack," Billy said.

"There's more," Honey Bunny pressed on, like a nutter trudging through an extra-long reading assignment. "The part that's got Aggy's tail in a knot and Oscar swimming in circles. The last part of the story is that Ernie Bowman so loved Clearwater that he hid treasure in the school, in a 'Loaded Stash' for times of trouble."

"Whoa!" Malcolm raised up on his hind legs. "Times of trouble?! Like now?" He should have known that Aggy would have this all figured out.

Tank had slowly been extending his neck out of his shell. "Yes, I know this part! I remember hearing about the Loaded Stash from Gertrude—she was the old turtle who used to be in my room," he explained to Malcolm, Jesse, and Billy. "You never got to meet her, but she was the one who perfected the scooter slingshot. Good greens, we used to rocket down that hall ..." His voice grew soft. He ducked into his shell. "She was legendary in her own way." From deep within, he cleared his throat. "But Gertrude always said that no one knew where the Loaded Stash was anymore. Or even *what* it was."

"Well, yes," Aggy said. "That's kind of where we're at. The details have been ... lost to time."

Tank edged his head back out. "Zapped by Skylar, is how Gertrude put it."

Malcolm's attention had been zinging about the circle of critters almost as fast as a scooter slingshot. Knacks! Silver dogs! Loaded Stashes! But . . . "Skylar? From my Room 11?"

Aggy nodded. "Yes. When Skylar was in kindergarten, there was a little accident with Oscar's aquarium."

Oscar nudged around in his gravel. "ALMOST DIED."

"Anyway, we lost a great deal. The lankies threw out most of our historical records, and the sole computer that we had been keeping files on was . . . drowned."

"Then Octavius came," Harriet said. "He brought us up to speed, and we went to computer files in the cloud." The spider saluted.

"But even before that," Aggy continued, "our records were a little . . . whimsical.[2] You see, before computers, everything was told critter to critter. You know our Marks?" Malcolm pictured the symbols the Academy scratched throughout the building to communicate safe places or danger. "That's how Marks came to be," she explained. "They were like signposts, really. Markers to remind critters of a bigger story. And the problem with oral records is that—"

"It depends on who's telling them," Honey Bunny

---

[2] Whimsical = unpredictable, unusual, playful. Vocabulary from 1/19. (Not a typical kindergarten vocabulary word—how did Aggy know?) Sometimes Skylar's math facts were a little . . . whimsical.

finished. "Even that Ernie Bowman story. If Harriet had shared it, likely she would have told it differently."

"That's for sure," Harriet said under her breath.

Honey Bunny's hind foot started tapping again. "So, I still don't see what you think we're going to do with this, Aggy. Save the school with this Loaded Stash? Even if this story was true — which I can't say I agree with — we don't have enough information. We don't know where or what to look for!" He lowered his voice. "Aggy, you know I respect your ideas. But I think this is so serious, we need to focus on something practical."

She whirled about then, and Malcolm had to leap out of the way of her flying tail. The folds of scales beneath her chin flared. Malcolm had never seen her so . . . What was it? Angry? Desperate? Frustrated? Or maybe a combination of all of them. "Practical?" She snorted. "Honey Bunny, have you heard anything that's been reported back in the last year from the district? What's practical *is* closing the building. It's too old, outdated, worn-out, and expensive!"

Honey Bunny closed his mouth, his ears drooping. Harriet sucked in her breath and groomed her spines. Even Pete's eye stalks turned away.

But not Malcolm. He twisted his tail, thinking hard. Yes, the story was skimpy and difficult to believe, but the truth was that Aggy was the one critter who had always stood by him, even when everyone had thought he was a skuzzy rat. And if Aggy believed this was all they had to save the school, then Malcolm was in. Maybe Jesse would say that was his hero brain talking, but he owed Aggy this, no matter how crazy it sounded.

He cleared his throat. He very rarely addressed the whole Academy, but now he was about to. "I think we should look into it." He scuffed his rear claws, then looked up. "After all, what do we have to lose?"

CHAPTER 6
THE DICTIONARY NICHE

"Thank you, Malcolm. Now follow me." Without wait-ing to hear the Academy's response, Aggy lumbered to the edge of the counter and slipped of into the darkness. Honey Bunny watched her go and blew out a long breath. He glared at Oscar. "Did you put her up to this? What's this all about?"

Oscar swished his fins. The gravel in the bottom of his aquarium was now in the shape of an arrow. Pointing in the direction Aggy had just disappeared in.

"Come on, HB," Malcolm urged. "Just give it a chance."

"It's not that I don't support her," Honey Bunny grum-bled as he followed Malcolm to the edge of the counter. "I do. She's gotten us through more scrapes than even the state math team could count. But I don't want her to get her hopes up. This all is so *unlikely*."

Polly glided down to land next to Honey Bunny. "Maybe hopes are what she needs right now."

"But—" Polly cocked her head and Honey Bunny sighed. "Aw, crumb. Maybe you're right." He grabbed a small flashlight with his mouth.

The group made their way over to where Aggy paced near the reference bookcases. Honey Bunny clicked on the flashlight, and Malcolm saw fluffs of dust waft with each sweep of Aggy's tail. Gristle, how long had it been since some of the books had been taken out? Then he spied a familiar one on the bottom shelf.

"Hey, my dictionary!" He took a deep whiff of the musty, dusty old paper smell. You couldn't tell from looking at it, but the dictionary was hollow on the inside. Malcolm had stayed there for a bit when he had kind of bitten Amelia and couldn't go back to Room 11. It was no three-story deluxe cage with a Comf-E-Cube, tail-safe exercise wheel, and an antibacterial water bottle, but it had been comfortable. And warm. And safe. Which is really all you can ask of from a home.

He reached out and traced a shape scratched into its spine. An Academy Mark, one of those "signposts" that Aggy had been talking about earlier. "What does this one mean, again?" he asked. "'Dwell here'?"

Aggy nodded. "That's really where it began." She looked up. "Do you remember last fall when we found this Mark? It perplexed us. We thought we knew all the Marks of the building. But here was a new one. Or, should we say, a very old one. So I decided to take a little closer look."

With her tail, she shoved the dictionary off the shelf. It fell open, revealing the cozy little space Malcolm had lived in. But Aggy didn't stop there. She knocked the rest of the row of books off the shelf too.

"Cheez, Aggy. I'm not sure Mrs. Snyder's going to like this," Jesse said.

"I'm not just making a mess. Look." She stepped back.

The critters leaned forward. Behind all the books was a narrow cabinet door built into the wall. Aggy hooked her tail through the handle and gave a tug. The door popped open.

A dark space yawned before them. The stale air swirled out, reminding Malcolm of the closed fourth floor.

Jesse did a cartwheel. "The Loaded Stash!" he crowed.

Honey Bunny aimed his light inside. The cabinet was crammed with piles of springs from ballpoint pens, bits of shoelaces, old magazines, a stash of pop tabs, and more. Junk. A blue feather drifted out.

Billy groaned. "More like a load of *trash*. What is this place?"

"It's a Niche," Polly said, flittering to the shelf above it and peering in upside down. "Isn't it?"

Aggy nodded. "I think the cabinet itself was an electrical panel at one time. Or something. It's not Academy handiwork. But the stuff inside? Yes, Oscar and I think it's an old Niche—a place where the Academy collects little bits and bobs from the lankies and nutters. Things they won't notice missing, but might help us in our work.[1] This one's clearly been here for ages, forgotten. I haven't explored the whole thing—I don't quite fit—but there was something just inside the door that made me"—she turned to Honey Bunny and winked—"get my hopes up."

"Oh, come on, Aggy," Honey Bunny protested. "You heard that?" He muttered under his breath, "I thought reptiles weren't supposed to have a good sense of hearing."

"What was that?" asked Aggy.

"Never mind. What did you find inside?"

"Malcolm, perhaps you would be so kind as to fetch it?"

"Me?" Malcolm jumped a little. "Sure." He crawled in, blinking to let his eyes adjust.

When he did, he was face-to-face with a mouse! Or a pink, fuzzy, mousy-like stuffed toy—a lot like what they sold in the Pet Emporium. Beyond that, there was a stack of magazines, some comics, a couple catalogs. But that couldn't be what Aggy was talking about. Who would get excited about "menswear" from 1935? This Niche was a jumble—as messy as the inside of Skylar's desk! He stuck his head out. "What exactly am I fetching?"

---

[1] The Academy handbook has a whole section on various uses of "tools" found at school—usually found in Ms. Brumble's swept-up piles at the end of the day.

"Next to the papers," Aggy urged. "You'll see."
Malcolm sniffed around the comics and catalogs and come
to a hoard of paper clips and a single coin.

Well, paper clips were paper clips, no matter what year
they were from. So Malcolm pushed the coin back out into
the light.

It dropped off the cabinet's door ledge and rolled to the center of the Academy members, spinning for a moment. It fell over flat with a quick flash in the dim light.

When it did, every member of the Midnight Academy gasped. Pete clacked his claws dangerously close to Honey Bunny's ears. "Great greens!" he said, gulping.

Malcolm pushed his way through to see what everyone else was so excited about. But it was just a coin. A small silver coin, not unlike the ones his nutters had every day in their pockets and desks and backpacks.

Honey Bunny's mouth was gaping. "Well, why didn't you say so before?" he asked Aggy. "Why all the dramatics?"

"Would you have believed me?" She smiled.

"What? What?" Malcolm asked. Suddenly, a thought hit him. "Oh! The coin is worth a lot, isn't it? Is it enough to keep the school running? Repair the electrical?"

There was a moment of silence—then Polly twittered. Honey Bunny chuckled. And Billy and Jesse actually clung to each other as they laughed at Malcolm. He felt the soles of his feet blush.

"I'm sorry, Malcolm," Aggy said, gasping for breath. "But no. This is a nickel. Five cents. You can't even buy milk in the cafeteria for that much."

"Oh, it's not just a nickel," Honey Bunny said. "Look what's on it. Look closely. See anything different?"

Malcolm stepped closer. On the face of the coin was a

dog. Some kind of hound, with his tongue hanging out. Malcolm shrugged. "I . . . still don't get it."

"Pinched parsley, rat, have you never seen a nickel before?" Harriet broke in impatiently.

"No, not exactly," Malcolm admitted.

Honey Bunny explained, "Most nickels don't look like that, even old ones from"—he glanced at the coin—"1935. No, someone carved into that coin. And they carved a *dog* . . . on a *silver* nickel."

"'Dogs into silver'!" Malcolm said with Honey Bunny. "But if that part of the legend is real, that means . . ." Malcolm continued.

"The rest of the story could be true too," finished Aggy. "Maybe there *is* a Loaded Stash out there. It certainly seems more likely, knowing that this coin exists. And if there is a Loaded Stash, well, we need it."

A flutter of hope pulsed in Malcolm's chest. Yes, maybe there *was* something that the Midnight Academy could do. What did they have—three weeks? Why, anything could happen in three weeks.

And then Malcolm remembered something else. Maybe it was Honey Bunny saying that year, 1935. But he asked, "Did you mention before that Ernie Bowman always wore red suspenders?"

Honey Bunny nodded. Malcolm bounded back into the Niche. He tugged on the stack of magazines and comics, pulling the top one free. Then he dragged it with his teeth to the door and out to the center of the circle of critters. "Is this what suspenders look like?"

Honey Bunny aimed the flashlight at the pages. It was an ad on the back of an old magazine.

"Color! Style! Comfort! Your choice of suspenders in five new models. 45¢."

"Those are suspenders?" Jesse peeped at the picture.

"Cheez, those look uncomfortable," Billy commented.

"If you ask me, all clothes look uncomfortable," said Polly. "How about the way nutters tie up their feet in shoes? Or put mittens over the ends of their wings?" She shook her head. "It's a miracle they can do anything!"

Pete waggled his shell. "Oh, wearing something isn't so bad. Not if it keeps you safe and warm. Right, Tank?"

The critters buzzed and laughed.

Finally, Honey Bunny set the flashlight on the floor. "Um, I hate to say it, but . . . what do we do now?"

Harriet groaned. "Oh, don't start that again!"

"No, no," Aggy said. "It's a legitimate question. And actually, Harriet, I think you had a very wise response before."

"Was that the one where we don't do anything?" Billy asked. "We sit around and wait?"

"Well, yes. But now we have so many more things on which to train our Midnight Academy eyes, ears, noses, and whiskers. Or in my case . . . a Jacobson's organ and a parietal eye[2]—but those never seem to make it into the handbook," she murmured. "Anyway"—she stepped into the flashlight's beam—"tomorrow, not only do I want you to pay attention to your nutters' and lankies' reactions to this news, but we all also need to be watchful for niblets of Ernie Bowman's legend." She gestured with her tail. "Apparently, it's been among us for years, and we never knew it. Now that it's fresh in our minds, though, we might find we know more than we realize. Maybe it's a reference to a bird, or a long-hidden Mark under some paint, or . . . well, I can't for the life of me think of what that wish-granting one could be. But let's be on our watch tomorrow and the next day. Then we'll keep our regular meeting on Thursday. Come prepared to share."

---

[2] It's true—iguanas have a third eye on the top of their head! You can't really see it, but it senses light and predators. And Aggy can also smell through her Jacobson's organ in her mouth. Who knew?

CHAPTER 7
ALL-STARS

The next morning, Malcolm was primed and ready to go. McKenna needed saving? A legend needed uncovering? He was the rat to do it.

Unfortunately, it was 6:30 a.m., and he had a rather long wait until you or the nutters arrived, Mr. Binney.

Amelia, as usual, was the first one in. She wore a green fleece hooded sweatshirt with matching green socks, and her black hair was pulled smoothly back into a green elastic band. She set her stack of folders and notebooks down (also color-coordinated, according to the subject) at the table she shared with Malcolm, gave him a little scratch through his wire cage, and proceeded to write the vocabulary word of the day on the dry-erase board. This was a task that you used to do, Mr. Binney, but, like keeping the calendar up-to-date and alphabetizing the classroom library, it was simply more efficient to put Amelia in charge.

"PERSEVERANCE," she wrote. "Sticking with something, even after it gets hard."

Malcolm watched her dot the i's and cross the t's. Did she pick that word on purpose?

His question was answered by the newspaper article she pulled out of her binder. "Did you hear?" she whispered. "They want to close our school."

Malcolm longed for her to pull him out of his cage. He had so much to tell her. And ask her! After all, Amelia was smart—she might know something of the legend. But then you came in, Mr. Binney, and the rest of the fifth-graders, and all Amelia could do was scratch Malcolm again and say, "Lunchtime, okay? We'll talk then."

As the rest of the students poured through the door, Malcolm stood up on his hind legs and pressed his nose to the edge of his cage. He felt a surge of pride and love for his nutters: some sleepy, some shouting, some a little damp from the slushy puddles out on the playground. How could the school board close this? Skylar, trying to put his shoes on the wrong feet. Tianna, slicking on berry-berry lip gloss while blowing an enormous bubble of watermelon-burst gum. Kiera, treating everyone to an encore performance of "Rocky Top." Michael, trying to forge his mom's signature on his reading log. (You already knew about that, right, Mr. Binney? Whose mom writes in colored pencil!)

Jovahn, whose sneakers were probably the dampest because he had just won the impromptu[1] puddle-jumping contest (nine feet and, more important, a huge splash that made it all the way over to the fourth-graders' line), pinwheeled into the classroom. Malcolm's ears perked up and—he was embarrassed to notice—his stomach rumbled.

Jovahn dropped his binder on his desk with a bang, then headed over to Malcolm's cage, like he usually did. Malcolm raised his paws up in anticipation.

"Hey, mousie!" Jovahn teased.

"Stop it!" Amelia scolded. Malcolm sniffed and pretended to hide behind his antibacterial water bottle.

"Oh, come on, you two. I was kidding! Look at that tail. That magnificent ratty tail!" Jovahn said. "Come on, here's breakfast." He held out a pinch of Pop-Tart that he had saved in his pocket. Malcolm crept out, his whiskers twitching as he took the snack.

Crumb, it was good. Blueberry, his favorite. Still, Malcolm gently nipped Jovahn's finger as he took it—

---

[1] Impromptu = spur of the moment. Vocabulary from 12/17. Most of Jovahn's day—from puddle-jumping to flinging french fries at lunch—could be considered impromptu.

a little payback. Jovahn smiled at the joke and rubbed Malcolm behind the ears.

"Okay, class." You flicked the lights to get everyone's attention, Mr. Binney. "Great work last night. I heard Mrs. Findlay say that it turned out to be one of the best musicals she's ever directed. So, nice job. I'm glad you pulled it together." You settled on your tall stool at the front of the room. "There's something else I want to talk to you about, though. I know some of you have heard that the school board met last night." You took a deep breath. "There's a possibility that McKenna might close next year."

Michael set his colored pencil down and leaned back in his chair until Malcolm was sure it would tip over. "My dad says it's already decided. McKenna's done for. Us fifth-graders will be the last class to graduate."

Amelia smoothed the clipped article out on top of her binder. "That's not what the newspaper said. The newspaper said that *we* fifth-graders, along with everyone else, don't know yet."

Jovahn agreed. "My mom says we should do something as a class for those listening sessions." He raised his eyebrows in a question at Amelia.

Tianna cracked her gum. "Who cares? We're fifth-graders. We're out of here anyway at the end of the school year."

Malcolm frowned. There it was again. Yesterday it had been you, Mr. Binney, who had mentioned something like that: "*. . . before this bunch is ready to leave McKenna for middle school.*" What was that about? Crumb, he really had a lot to talk about with Amelia today.

"My family cares," Kiera said, putting down her note. She hardly ever disagreed with Tianna, so Malcolm slowed down a little on his exercise wheel. "My little sister's in second grade. If they close the school, she won't get to see her friends anymore. They'll go to Fairfax, and she'll have to ride the bus twice as long to Parkview. We *should* do something."

Skylar looked up from his shoes. "My Gram went to school here. She says it's a shame they're letting the school get so run-down."

"Why should they spend the money if there's room for us at other schools?" Jenna asked. She shrugged. "That's what my dad says."

And the conversation rolled on. Some nutters felt deeply about it. Others were more concerned about the hot lunch menu for the day.

Finally, you held up your hand and waited for quiet. "Okay, obviously not everyone agrees. But here's your chance to do something about it. I've spoken with our principal, Mrs. Rivera. She and I both feel strongly that a school is more than a building and that this one needs to stay open. We also believe this is not insurmountable. We're wondering: Would any of you want to work on a presentation of sorts for the first listening session? Show them a student's point of view. What do you think?"

The class grew quiet. Skylar, of all people, raised his hand. "I'll do it. My Gram says someone should talk about the history of the school. How it was named after Walton McKenna. He was a lumber baron—she said that was like a boss. Really rich. Our school was called Clearwater Central High School until the 1930s, when he donated money and land for them to build the gym and auditorium. Then they called it McKenna High School. It didn't become an elementary school until much later, after they built the high school."

The whole class, Malcolm and Amelia included, stared at Skylar. This was maybe the most he had ever said all school year—and definitely the most he had ever said that actually made sense.

Even you struggled to keep the surprise out of your voice. "Wow—yes, Skylar. I think I've heard that before. And your Gram has a good idea, I think. Many in the community will have fond memories of our school. It might be good to remind them. Anyone else?"

Kiera raised her hand. "I will."

"Me too," Amelia said.

"Great. Jovahn, do you want to join in? Put that shoe on, then, instead of waving it around." You made a note and looked at the list. "Well, you should be quite an all-star team. When we go to the library later, why don't you four get together and we can talk about what you'd like to do. For now, though, let's get out our math notebooks . . ."

The rest of the morning zoomed by. Malcolm might

have taken a small nap, because all of the sudden Amelia was opening his cage and, with a well-practiced motion, slipped him into her green hood. The rest of the class was busy banging their desks closed, washing up at the sink, and heading out of the room. Lunchtime.

"You coming?" Jovahn waited for Amelia in the doorway.

Amelia nodded. "Sure." She started down the hall with the rest of the fifth-graders, then paused. "Oh, hey, I'm going to run to the restroom. I'll meet you down there."

Jovahn shrugged. "Okay." And he jogged to catch up with the rest of the class without looking back. Not Kiera,[2] though. Malcolm peeked out of Amelia's hood just in time to catch her spying on them as Amelia slipped into the bathroom.

To be honest, Malcolm didn't quite understand what Amelia was up to either. While not exactly as motivated by food as Malcolm or Jovahn, she still had always been a girl who had at least enjoyed lunch. But for the last three weeks, she had pulled this bathroom trick. Not every day, but maybe once or twice a week. She'd start out by going with the class down to lunch, then slip away to the restroom. The weird thing was, she never ended up going back to the cafeteria. She'd stay until the end of lunch recess, holed up in the bathroom. And—most baffling of all—she never had anything to eat. When the bell rang, she'd

---

[2] If nutters did have Knacks, then Kiera's might be a super-sense for secrets of any kind.

slip into the pack of milling kids in the hallway. Malcolm couldn't figure it out. But at the same time, he wasn't sure he wanted to, either. Because Amelia always brought him along. And it was forty minutes of time they got to spend together—time they didn't otherwise have.

Once in the girls' bathroom, Amelia headed for the last stall. It was a double-wide one from which the toilet had been removed long ago. Now, instead, it had a bench under its frosted window. Strange, but McKenna was an old school, and, honestly, as far as Malcolm was concerned, you could find anything behind the doors of McKenna.

Amelia set Malcolm down on the bench, then pulled a well-worn notebook and a *Merriam-Webster's* student dictionary out of her backpack. He stepped onto the notebook. He poised his tail. "So much to tell you," he spelled out.

Remember how Malcolm's Knack was learning to read without learning to read, Mr. Binney? Well, for quite some time, Amelia had kept his secret. And between the student dictionary and this notebook with the letters of the alphabet all spaced out, Malcolm could tell Amelia anything. And he did. His rat tail made the perfect pointer.

Of course, whenever something big happened, like last night, it was a little exhausting for him to—literally —spell it all out for Amelia.

But at least they had a forty-minute lunch break.

"No kidding." Amelia's brown-black eyes widened twenty minutes later. "A Loaded Stash? Are you serious?" She had brought a couple of graham crackers from the classroom snack cupboard, and she passed him a corner.

Malcolm was lying on the notebook now, panting. He pointed. "But we don't know where to look." He took the cracker.

"Hmmm." Amelia leaned back against the wall and drew her feet up on the bench. She twisted the end of her ponytail while nibbling absently on a cracker (she'd make a very good rat, Malcolm thought proudly). "If it were me, I'd ask everyone I know. All the critters."

"We have. Everyone was at the meeting."

"Not *everyone*," she said.

Malcolm looked at her quizzically.

She gestured wide. "There's a whole world outside these walls, you know. Other schools, other . . . places to live, even. You've seen a glimpse of it at the pet store. But even in this school, there must be other critters around. Maybe even some who have been around longer than you pets. You should talk to them."

Malcolm considered. Amelia was right. There was his friend Beert, the "ghost of McKenna"—otherwise known as the barn owl who used to be trapped in the clock tower. And Sylvia, too. Maybe she knew more than rodent rules and how to care for squirrelings. Didn't she say her nest was seventh generation? Just because they weren't Midnight Academy members didn't mean they didn't know a piece of the story. They simply might not know that they knew. If that made sense.

"Thanks, Amelia. Don't know what I'd do without you," Malcolm spelled, then scrambled up onto her knees.

Amelia gave him half a smile, scooped him up, and snuggled him under her chin.

Crumb, it was the truth. Malcolm hoped things would always stay exactly as they were—Amelia and him together forever.

CHAPTER 8
YEARBOOKS

Later that afternoon, the fifth-graders of Room 11 con-
verged on the library. As soon as they entered, they spread
out, most looking for books to read, but some for a hidden corner to visit with friends—you know about that,
right, Mr. Binney? Amelia kind of fell into both categories.
She settled at a table near Oscar's aquarium and cracked
open *Mrs. Frisby and the Rats of NIMH*. After a moment, she
pulled the green elastic band out of her hair, and Malcolm[1]

---

[1] We know you said he had to stay in his cage, and usually Amelia is such a
good listener. But sometimes there's hearing and sometimes there's listening.
And sometimes there's hearing *and* listening, but doing what you need at the
time anyway.

crept from her hood to her shoulder. He was dying to find out if the rats escaped the rosebush!

But before they could get started, Kiera strolled up and Malcolm had to dive for cover. "Where were you at lunch, Amelia?"

Jovahn's attention had been zoomed in on the cars section, but he paused after hearing this. "Yeah . . . you never came back."

"Oh . . ." Amelia waved her hand as if to erase the conversation. "I didn't feel well, so I went down to the office. All better now, though." Deep in the hood, Malcolm frowned and bit a whisker. Since when had Amelia become such a good liar? Then she cleared her throat. "So, after you get your books, maybe we should talk about the school board presentation like Mr. Binney said?"

Kiera shrugged. "Sure—give me a minute."

Amelia settled back with her book. She flicked through a few pages, but Malcolm knew she wasn't really reading. Finally, she set it down and glanced over at the reference shelves. "Is that it, Malcolm?" she whispered. "Is that your dictionary? And the shelf?" And before Malcolm could even squeak an answer, she stood up and headed over to it. Oscar splashed as they zoomed by.

At the shelf, Amelia knelt down. She pulled the giant dictionary toward her.

From across the room, Mrs. Snyder, the librarian, called out, "Oh, Amelia, dear, that can't be checked out."

"I know," answered Amelia. "I just wanted to look up a word."

"Well, depending on what it is, you might have better luck with one of our online dictionaries," Mrs. Snyder said. "That one hasn't been used in ages."

"Or since last fall," Amelia whispered so that only Malcolm could hear. She traced the shape scratched on the spine of the book. "So, this is a Mark, huh?"

Malcolm, who had crept back to the top of Amelia's hood to peer over her shoulder, nodded. He watched as Amelia felt the wall behind the bookcase and, with a little tug, popped open the cabinet door.

Malcolm raced under her hair to her other shoulder. He darted a look left and right. What was she doing?! Oscar gave another splash, but the rest of the class seemed safely occupied. At the circulation desk, Mrs. Snyder was now arguing with Skylar, trying to explain the difference between re*new*ing a book and re*turn*ing a book.

Amelia reached in. When she pulled her hand out, the coin with the dog carving was in it. She pinched it between her thumb and forefinger and studied it. "Yeah, that's weird, all right." She flipped it over. "1935."

"Where'd you get that?" Malcolm jumped at the sound of Jovahn's voice. Where had he come from?

Amelia paused. "It's, uh, kind of a long story."

Jovahn raised his eyebrows and knelt down next to her. "Like write-it-all-out-in-a-book long?" he asked. Jovahn was one of the only nutters who knew everything about Malcolm and the Midnight Academy. Then he spied Malcolm. "Hey," he whispered.

Malcolm waved back, but Amelia shrugged. "I don't know yet. I'll tell you about it later." Then she bent down so she was eye level with the bottom shelf. "Hey—look!" She shoved the dictionary back on the shelf and grabbed a different book. It was thick, but not dictionary thick. It seemed to be full of photographs. She scanned for a moment, then pulled several other books off the shelf. "Come on!"

Jovahn trotted behind her back to the table. "What? What is it?"

But she didn't answer. Instead she thumped the books down on the table where Skylar and Kiera had gathered. "Yearbooks," she crowed. "Skylar, remember your Gram's idea about talking about the history of the school? Well . . ." She opened a book dramatically to a spread. "How about we *show* them? McKenna through the years. We can scan pictures from these yearbooks. From when McKenna was a high school. They go all the way back."

Kiera peered at the page and squealed. "Ew—look at their glasses! And their hair." She flipped the cover. "What year is this, anyway? Do they have any recent ones? With us in them?"

"Probably, but I think we should show the history. That's 1952," Amelia answered, pointing to the year on the cover. "I'm looking in . . . 1935." Malcolm's ears perked up. He knew she hadn't picked that year off the shelf by coincidence. Amelia never did anything by coincidence. He watched as she flipped to the back of the book and ran her finger down the list of staff members. *Colin Bertram, Mathematics. Miriam Bothelsby, Home Economics. Franklin Carter, Chemistry.* She closed the yearbook, picked up another, and did the same. Malcolm suppressed a grin. Amelia was searching for Ernie Bowman!

The group of four flipped through the books for a moment. "Sweet—they had a small engines class in 1979," Jovahn said. He sighed dreamily. "They taught *automotive arts.*" Then he put his finger in the book. "What are we looking for, exactly, anyway?"

"Pictures. Anything sentimental," Amelia said, scanning another index.

"What's 'sentimental'?" asked Skylar. He was chewing on the end of a pencil and staring at the bank of windows in the back of the library. A group of students had gathered there.

"'Sentimental' means sappy," Kiera answered. "Oooo—" She sat up. "They elected a Clearwater Queen each year."

Amelia snorted softly. "That's sappy, all right." She turned a page, read for a bit, then leaned forward so fast, Malcolm was almost knocked from her shoulder. "Like this!" She shoved her yearbook to the center of the table and jabbed at it. "In 1938, when they built the auditorium and gym addition, they buried a *time capsule*." She looked around. "This is it, All-Stars! We could open it for the board meeting. How dramatic would that be? There's nothing more sentimental than a time capsule!"

"Look ... there's—" Skylar said, pointing toward the window.

Jovahn interrupted. "What's a time capsule, again?"

Amelia gestured impatiently. "You know, a container of stuff from that time period. There's usually a big ceremony when they bury it, and later you dig it up to see what it was like back then. It's perfect."

Malcolm looked through Amelia's hair to the black-and-white photo that had gotten her so excited. A group of students circled a man holding a metal box. Everyone was beaming, even the dog in the corner with his tongue hanging out. Malcolm read, "Walton McKenna, town benefactor and patron of the new school auditorium, watches on with pride as the materials for the time capsule are gathered. The capsule will be placed under the Council Oak tree when the addition is finished."

"What's a 'Council Oak'?" Jovahn asked.

But Kiera tapped the page with a chipped purple-painted nail. "That's Walton McKenna. The boss Skylar said one our school is named after."

"Yeah," Amelia said. "That's what the caption says. That's what captions do." She turned to Jovahn. "I don't know. Let's ask Mr. Binney."

Kiera rolled her eyes at Amelia. "What I'm trying to say

is that I've seen that guy's picture before. There used to be a painting of him in the back of the auditorium. Talk about sentimental. We should show that with the time capule!"

"That's a good idea." Jovahn said, and poked Skylar. "But didn't you knock it off the wall in third grade?"

Skylar spun back around to face the group. He squirmed uncomfortably. "I got my foot caught in the seat. I was trying to get untangled, and my shoe accidentally—"

A horrible squawking noise, like a thousand desks being moved all at once across a tile floor, interrupted him. Michael was trying to pry a window open. "Look! Over there," someone said. Fifth-graders turned toward him.

Mrs. Snyder's head snapped up. She scurried around the desk. "We don't open those windows!"

More kids flocked over. Kiera set down her yearbook and joined them.

Then, over all the kids' voices and the old wooden window creaking open, a yowl. That's really the only way to describe it—a yowl. A yowl that made Jovahn lose his page on automotive arts and Amelia stiffen so that Malcolm fell down into the bottom of her hood. It sounded awful. Like sadness poured into anger and mixed with rusty nails.

"Is that a—" Amelia started. She stared at Jovahn.

"It sounds like—" he answered, but it was Skylar who finished.

"There's a cat in the tree outside."

"What?" Amelia stood up. Her chair knocked over. "Where?" She plowed through the group of fifth-graders, elbowing her way to the window. Malcolm, deep in her hood, wanted her both to go faster and to run away, all at the same time. She reached the window and leaned her forehead against the glass. "Where?" she asked again.

Michael pointed to a branch. "There. You see it?"

"No, I—"

But you pushed your way into the group then, Mr. Binney. "Okay, okay," you said, steering kids toward the door. "We've all seen a cat before. If you have time for this, you must all be checked out. Let's go. Line up."

The class started dispersing, but Amelia lingered. "It's gone," she whispered, and Malcolm knew that she was talking to him. "I didn't see it."

Jovahn stepped up. "Me either. All I saw was the white tip of its tail as it slipped behind the trunk. I couldn't see anything else."

"White tip?" Amelia repeated. Her voice shook a little. Subtly.[2] You probably couldn't notice unless you were also doing your own fair share of trembling deep in a green fleece hood. "A lot of cats have white-tipped tails. It could have been any cat."

She was right: it *could* have been any cat. But with a white-tipped tail, it also could have been a *certain* cat. A certain cat who had disappeared months ago yet still

---

[2] Subtly. From the word *subtle*, which was our actual vocabulary word from 12/14. Slight, a little, barely noticeable. Not to be rude, but Mrs. Findlay's perfume is anything but subtle. Seriously. It's a good thing Harriet and her allergies aren't in that room.

fueled Malcolm's imagination whenever he faced a shadowy corner.

Snip.

However unlikely, it could also have been her.

CHAPTER 9
THE STRIPED SHADOW

That night, the "what if's" were burning up Malcolm's brain. Logically, he knew that the cat probably wasn't Snip. She hadn't been seen in months, and like Amelia said, *lots* of cats had white-tipped tails.

But still.

Have you ever felt like that, Mr. Binney? When you know deep down that the worst likely isn't true—but yet you can't stop thinking: What if it *is?* And then that tiny sliver of possibility takes over your whole world.

If only there were someone to talk to. To dismiss all this. Jesse and Billy would only poke fun. And Aggy was so busy with her own worries. Malcolm paced back and forth in his cage, too agitated to even get on his tail-safe exercise wheel.

He tried to reassure himself. He had been all worked up over the shadow in the rafters, too, and that had turned out to be Sylvia and her squirrelings, not Snip. Then Malcolm paused, midstride. Maybe he should talk to *Sylvia*. Maybe she knew who the cat was. After all, the cat was outside and Sylvia was, as she put it, Outside. And then Malcolm could Know it was nothing. Then he could redirect his worries to what actually mattered: McKenna closing.

And before he could do another lap in his cage, Malcolm was out the door and down the hall to the auditorium.

Sylvia was almost exactly where Malcolm had left her —tucking her squirrelings in the tight space between the walls of the auditorium.

"Who's there!" she hissed, baring her teeth. "I will bite!"

Malcolm held up his tail. "It's me, Sylvia. Malcolm. Do you remember? From the other night? I won't hurt you."

She snarled, "Oh, I'm not afraid of that. But *I* will hurt *you* if you wake up these squirrelings." Then she saw Malcolm's face. "What's happened?"

Before Malcolm could answer, she held up a paw and pointed a claw. "Let's go where we can talk." She led him up through the wall. They wound through insulation and wiring and bits of paper. Then they squeezed through the hole in the bricks and popped out on the other side. She crouched on the slanted roof. "Now—what?"

"Whoa," Malcolm said, gazing out, his nose and whiskers positively twanging. The air was clear and cold, and the tree stretched its branches tantalizingly close. He reached out a paw. He could probably make it, if he took a running leap—

"Malcolm?" Sylvia pulled an acorn from a stash in the wall. She popped it into her cheek. "Have you ever been outside before?"

Malcolm nodded. "Well, sure. Yeah, a few times." He shrugged sheepishly. "Well, never like this. Usually when I've been outside, someone's . . . after me."

"Once you're Out, you're never In," she said, sitting back and sucking on the acorn.

Malcolm sat next to her. "I thought there were . . . Dangers on the Outside."

"Dangers can be worth it sometimes," she said, taking a deep breath and cracking into the acorn. She handed a piece of it to him.

"Well, that's kind of what I wanted to ask you about," Malcolm said, taking it. He sniffed. Nutty, like sunflower seeds. "Do you know what a cat is?"

She bounced a second acorn off his head, then caught it neatly on the rebound. "Of course! You might as well be asking me if I know what a maple is. There's not a squirrel alive that doesn't know about cats."

"Ow!" Malcolm rubbed his head. "Crumb, you can just say so, you know. We saw one today. In the tree outside the library. Do you know it?"

"The beech? Yes—fine, springy branches. Great for hide-and-seek. I'll be taking the squirrelings there later this spring."

"No, not the tree." Gristle, was she being difficult on purpose? "The cat." He stole a sideways glance at Sylvia and took a nibble of the acorn. Smoky and bitter, not unlike the air swirling around him.

She twitched her nose. "Sorry, can't help you. There are a few critters you don't want to get to know too well. Cats are at the top of the list. Cats, dogs, owls—oh, and cars. Definitely cars."

Malcolm nodded. He munched on the rest of his acorn. That was that, then. He was right back where he started. A sliver of worry.

Sylvia watched him. She reached out a paw and touched his shoulder. "Seriously, now. I wish I could help. What is this all about?"

Malcolm hesitated. What did an Outside squirrel— who was kind of a pain in the tail, to tell the truth—know about anything he was worried about? But sometimes, it doesn't matter what a person (or critter) knows. They just have to be willing to listen. And so, before he knew it, all of it poured out. Malcolm's nightmares about Snip, the hamsters' teasing, even the school closing and the fact that Amelia had been sneaking away and not eating lunch.

"Whoa," Sylvia said finally, after Malcolm had taken a breather. "The Outside may have Dangers, but I've got to say, it's simpler. Eat and try not to be eaten. That's about the extent of our worries."

It did sound wonderfully simple. But at the same time, Malcolm knew he could never give up all that he had Inside.

"You know . . ." she said. She picked up an acorn that had fallen out of the hole and twirled it about on its point for a minute. "I'm not sure if I should bring this up. I wonder . . ." The acorn wobbled and toppled on its side. "Sometimes when Outside critters have problems—bigger than 'eat and try not to be eaten'—they go to a . . . fixer of sorts."

Malcolm's head jerked up. "A 'fixer'?"

She picked up the acorn again. "More of a broker, really. Someone who . . . arranges things."

"What do you mean?" Malcolm tried to tamp down the little spark of hope he felt. This might be exactly what the Midnight Academy needed!

"He fixes critters' problems. Run out of nuts for the winter? Your branch blows down in a storm? These are problems that Outside critters deal with all the time. But every once in a while, for whatever reason, a problem is insurmountable. A critter is desperate. And that's when they seek out the Striped Shadow."

Insurmountable? Malcolm had heard that word before. Aggy—she had used it at the Tangerine meeting. And Mr. Binney had used it too. At the time, Malcolm hadn't known exactly what it meant, so he had looked it up in his dictionary. "Insurmountable, impossible to overcome." But none of them—Aggy, Mr. Binney, or the dictionary—had mentioned fixers.

The fur on Malcolm's neck prickled up. Then he asked, "The Striped Shadow? You mentioned him before—didn't you? Isn't he the one who set up your nest?" It was hard to imagine Sylvia desperate. "But does he solve Inside critter problems? What about problems involving nutters?"

Sylvia set the acorn down and started it spinning again. "That's the thing. I don't know." She swiped the acorn, and it spun faster. "And there's more. The Striped Shadow fixes things . . . but there's a price. There's always a price."

Malcolm hardly heard any of that. Crumb, this was better than anything Malcolm could have imagined. So what if it *was* Snip in the trees? His worries about her seemed as puny as Sylvia's acorn next to the giant tree's branches. A *fixer!* Who knew such critters existed? Malcolm's hind legs trembled in his effort not to start dancing. "Where do I find him? This Striped Shadow?"

"That's the other thing. He's definitely Outside. He lives . . ." She gestured beyond McKenna's roof, and the acorn fell from her paw. They watched as it rolled down and off the roof. ". . . across the river. How would you get there?"

But Malcolm already knew. Hadn't Amelia said? He needed to talk to *all* the critters. And next up was his friend Beert the owl. Beert could get him across the river.

Malcolm knew he would. Then he would talk with the Striped Shadow and—sweet niblets!—by Thursday's Midnight Academy meeting, their insurmountable problem could be solved!

"Thanks, Sylvia! You are the best." Malcolm felt like hugging her, but he was a little afraid she might gouge out his eyes. So instead, he patted her paw and backed slowly away. "Say hi to the squirrelings for me, okay? And next time, I'll bring you some Inside food. Have they ever had corn dogs?"

And with that, Malcolm was back down through the wall and into the halls of McKenna.

CHAPTER 10
TO THE FOURTH

As Malcolm skidded out of the auditorium, he decided there was no need to go back to Room 11. He'd go straight up to see Beert now! The timing was perfect. When it came to saving the school, why wait?[1]

Still, even though Malcolm was motivated, it didn't make him any less jumpy. So he might have been rushing through the cat-shaped shadows on the landing of the stairs—just a bit—when he rounded the corner and ran smack into Honey Bunny's rocklike (yet fuzzy) chest. He

---

[1] This was something that Malcolm and Jovahn had in common. Amelia, on the other hand, preferred to weigh the options. Come to think of it, she and Aggy would get along great.

hit him so hard, he flipped over backwards and thumped down two steps.

"Malcolm?" Honey Bunny peered down at him in the dark.

"HB?"

"What are you doing here?" Honey Bunny hopped down to where Malcolm lay sprawled out.

"Um . . ." Have you ever had a notion so fresh, so new, you were afraid to say it out loud, Mr. Binney? That was Malcolm right then. "I had an idea."

But Honey Bunny leaned in. "Really? Can I come too? Because I'm wandering. I can't sleep at night,[2] so I thought I might as well look for all that crazy stuff Aggy was talking about. The sooner we can either prove or disprove it, the better, I figure. But I'm not getting anywhere. What's your plan?"

Malcolm sat up. "You want to come with me?" He couldn't believe his luck. Another set of ears, eyes, nose, and whiskers! You know . . . just in case.

Honey Bunny nodded.

"Okay, well, I'm on my way up to the clock tower. There's a critter I want to talk to."

Honey Bunny's pink eyes widened. "The clock tower?"

Malcolm smoothed his whiskers. "Yeah. But it's not who you're thinking of." And he set off up the stairs before Honey Bunny could respond.

---

[2] Most people do not know this, but rabbits are nocturnal.

Together they bounded up the stairs. On the closed fourth floor, Malcolm led, weaving through the jungle of discarded student desks, broken chairs, and rusty filing cabinets. He felt braver already with Honey Bunny at his side. He *was* one big bunny.

But as they approached the wooden door to the tower, Malcolm paused. He looked sideways at the rabbit and asked, "Do you remember this place?"

Honey Bunny sniffed. "Like I could forget, rat."

Malcolm nodded. He couldn't either. The last time they both had been up here, they had fought ferociously —Honey Bunny believing Malcolm had betrayed the Academy and Malcolm believing the same of Honey Bunny. Honey Bunny had ended up with a broken leg.

The rabbit cleared his throat. "Hey, you know I don't blame you for that. We both thought we were doing the right thing. It could have easily gone the other way." He flexed his muscles. "It should have."

Malcolm laughed.

Then Honey Bunny got serious. "But luckily, it didn't. Because you were right."

Malcolm nodded and swallowed. "I've never said I'm sorry you fell, though."

Honey Bunny stretched his right rear leg. "We both came out of that with some battle scars," he said, nodding toward Malcolm's tattered left ear and the thin white line of a scar on Malcolm's nose. "Besides . . ." He grinned.

"You wouldn't believe the nosh you get when you're in a pink bunny cast!"

Malcolm laughed again. "HB," he started. "Do you ever think you see . . . Snip?" If there was any critter in the building who might still also be having nightmares about cats, it would be Honey Bunny. "Sometimes I think . . . maybe Snip's alive out there . . ."

Honey Bunny shook his head. "Billy mentioned you've been fretting about this. Snip's gone, Malcolm." He sighed. "We probably should have told you, but we didn't want to upset you at the time. You had been through so much. Snip did not survive, Malcolm," he said gently. "The lankies —they did find something in the boiler room after they cleaned up the water."

Malcolm was quiet. "There was a cat. Today. In the tree—"

"No, Malcolm. We've got real worries to think about. Snip is not one of them anymore. So, is this where you were taking me?"

Malcolm nodded. "Almost. We have to get inside." He started to duck under the door, then stopped. "How will you—"

But Honey Bunny was already springing down the hall. "Meet you on the other side," he called over his ears.

Malcolm slipped under the door. The bottom of the clock tower looked and smelled the same as it always did. Stacks and stacks of old paint cans, layers of dust, the stuffy scent of an unused space. And the graffiti. Words and letters everywhere. Painted on the walls, written on the steps in marker. Carved into the wooden support beams. Years and years of students, sneaking up here and leaving their own kind of Mark.

Honey Bunny hopped from behind the narrow set of wooden stairs that led up to the clock itself. "Okay, we're here. So who are we meeting, exactly?"

Malcolm pawed at his whiskers. Where to begin? Jovahn had told him once that sometimes it is not necessary to tell the whole story. Just enough of it. "A friend of mine. I want to . . . ask him something. Also, Amelia . . ." Malcolm paused. Oops, maybe this was another part to leave out—technically, he should not be talking to nutters; it was against the Midnight Academy bylaws. Honey Bunny probably suspected that Malcolm and Amelia still chatted, but there was no reason to bring it up if he didn't need to. "Well, it also occurred to me that there are other critters around here. And maybe we should ask them about the legend."

Honey Bunny grunted, considering. "That's a good idea, rat. Why didn't I think of it?"

Malcolm clamored up the worn wooden staircase. In the middle of the dark space, clockwork gears ground away. "Beert?" he called out. The tower room must have been magnificent at one time, but now only one window had glass; the rest were boarded up. However, what lankies couldn't tell (please don't let Ms. Brumble know, Mr.

Binney) is that one window had a loose board. Strategically loose, for midnight visits between two friends.

"Beert and I have this system worked out. We meet up here to chat sometimes." Malcolm had to yell a little over the clicking and whirring of the gears. He wiggled through a crack in the clockwork case. "You have to wait until midnight—" The clock started bonging.

Bong . . . bong . . . bong . . .

"Then if you press here . . ." He flipped a lever, and a different wheel started turning.

Honey Bunny flattened his ears at the noise. "So who's Beert, again? Hey, I thought this clock was broken! Isn't this on the long list of things not working in our school?"

But Malcolm was counting. ". . . eleven . . . twelve . . . *thirteen.*"

"Thirteen? It *is* broken," said Honey Bunny.

Malcolm shook his head. "It's our signal. I give the clock an extra bong, and Beert knows I'm up here. You remember Beert. He's the ghost of McK—" But before he could finish, a shadow flashed across the sole glass window. A screech echoed through the night.

Honey Bunny lurched left and right, trying to hide. "Malcolm, look out! Get down!"

CHAPTER 11
A FAVOR

Malcolm peeked out around the clockwork case at the window. He waved to the shape outside. "It's okay, HB. *That* is Beert. He's a barn owl, but he won't hurt us, I promise. He's my friend."

Honey Bunny was frozen in place, using every bunny instinct to not be noticed. He panted. "He's what?! That's not *natural*, Malcolm. Owls eat critters like us!"

Malcolm nodded. "I know, but not *us*. Trust me. He sounds and looks a lot more terrifying than he is. He loves to swoop and scare people with his call."

"No kidding." There were white rings around the pink of Honey Bunny's eyes.

Malcolm scampered up to the windowsill. "Beert?"

Another screech—really almost a scream—reverberated through the tower. A white feather drifted down. Then a rustle at one of the boarded-up windows, and an owl beak poked through the strategic loose board. "Malcolm?" Beert's low rumble of a voice sounded completely different from the screams a moment ago.

"Beert! It's great to see you," Malcolm said, running up.

"Did you hear that last call of mine?" The owl pushed himself all the way through the hole, and Honey Bunny whimpered. "I scared the shorts off a late-night jogger—oh! We've got company." He twisted his head at Honey Bunny.

Honey Bunny opened his mouth, but nothing came out.

"That's Honey Bunny—HB," Malcolm said. "You might have seen him up here before?"

"He's a rabbit? Starlit skies, would you look at that. He's the color of the full moon." Beert clacked his beak. "He sure wouldn't last long Outside looking like that."

A small moan seeped out of Honey Bunny.

"He's from the Midnight Academy," Malcolm said quickly. Maybe he should change the subject. "Anyway, I have something to ask you."

The owl bowed his head down. "Anytime, Malcolm. You know that. Every night my Hestia says thanks for you." With a quick glance at Honey Bunny, Beert lowered his voice to a whisper. "We're having more owlets—did I tell you? Sometime later this spring."

Malcolm grinned. "That's wonderful."[1]

"So . . ." Beert fluffed out his wings. "What can I do for you?"

"Well, we're—" Malcolm nodded at Honey Bunny.

---

[1] Snip—this is almost too horrible to write—is the reason Beert and Hestia lost their first nest of owlets. It is possible that Malcolm is not the only critter at McKenna who still dreamed of Snip.

"The Academy, that is, is trying to track down an old story. About a man named Ernie Bowman. You ever heard of him?"

Beert slowly shook his head.

"How about wishes, or dogs turning into silver, or birds coming back to life? Loaded Stashes?"

"'Birds coming back to life'?" Beert repeated. "No. I wish I did. What is this about, Malcolm?"

"We're in trouble, Beert. The school and the Academy. They want to close McKenna, and we're trying everything we can to figure out a way to stop it. Everything." Malcolm paused. "So . . . there is one more thing . . ." He shot a glance at Honey Bunny. "You

know the Outside, right, Beert? I mean, you fly every-where."

Beert nodded. "Across the river, even all the way down to the dam. I know the skies above Clearwater."

"Do you know the critters, too?"

Beert folded his wings back and cocked his head. "Some. But not all. When you hunt, you aren't always introduced to everyone."

Malcolm swallowed. *Here goes.* "How about a critter called . . . 'the Striped Shadow'?"

"The Striped Shadow?" Beert took a step back. He coughed, almost like a bark. "Where did an Inside critter like you hear of *him?*"

Yes! Beert knew him! "Can you take me to him?"

But instead of answering, Beert turned to Honey Bunny. "Was this your idea? Is this why you're here?"

A quiver ran through Honey Bunny at being directly addressed by the owl, but he fought off instinct and said, "This is the first I've heard of it or him." His voice ended in a squeak that Malcolm knew was deeply embarrassing.

Beert turned back to Malcolm. "You don't want to mix up with him, Malcolm. Surely your Academy can help you instead."

"I just told you. It's *for* the Academy—the whole school," Malcolm pleaded. "Come on, I need to talk to him."

Beert shook his head and another white feather drifted

to the floor. "I don't know. Inside critters and Outside critters don't mix. You don't understand our rules."

Malcolm felt that same helplessness tangle in him again. "Why does everyone keep saying that? It's all we've got. *They're going to close the school,*" he nearly shouted. "Then where will we be?"

Beert flapped his wings. He opened his beak, then shut it. "You already took something from him?"

"What? No." What was Beert talking about?

"Wait." Honey Bunny stepped out of the shadows now. There was still a rim of white fear around his eyes, and he kept darting glances at Beert, but his voice was back to normal. "Who exactly is this 'Striped Shadow'? Why does Malcolm not want to mix up with him?" He turned to Malcolm. "And why do you always mix up with critters without checking with the Academy first? We probably have a file on this Shadow guy!"

Malcolm opened his mouth to protest, but before he could, Beert spoke up. "The Striped Shadow is a . . . helper for Outside animals. He provides aid when they're desperate."

"See?" Malcolm said to Honey Bunny. "He helps. Like the Midnight Academy!"

But Honey Bunny wasn't listening to Malcolm. He took a step closer to Beert. "What's the catch?" he asked him.

"The catch?"

"The catch," Honey Bunny repeated. "If he's such a

'helper,' well, then, why don't you want Malcolm to meet him?"

Beert coughed again. "The 'catch' is that he always—*always*—asks for payment. He doesn't do favors out of kindness." Beert turned to Malcolm. "He is not like the Midnight Academy."

A wiggle of fear rippled through Malcolm's middle. A feeling not unlike when you eat more corn chips than you should. But Malcolm tried to swallow it down. "It's our *school*," he said to Honey Bunny. "Aren't some things worth it?"

He turned to Beert and continued. "And, you—think of how you felt when you were separated from Hestia. What would you have done to get her back? Would you have asked for help from the Striped Shadow if you hadn't been trapped in the clock tower?"

Beert blinked his dark eyes. A long moment passed, and then slowly he unfolded his wing and extended it to Malcolm. Malcolm looked at Honey Bunny for a second, then crawled up to Beert's back. He snuggled down behind his head.

"Malcolm," Honey Bunny started. He looked so small next to the gears of the clock grinding away. "I . . . be careful," he finally said. "I wish I could go instead of you." He spoke to Beert next. "Bring him back. I'll wait here."

Beert nodded, then called back to Malcolm. "Hold on."

And they squeezed through the hole in the window and dropped off the side of the clock tower.

CHAPTER 12

UNDER the STARS

They rocketed down until Malcolm was sure that every niblet he had eaten for dinner that night *and* the night before was going to come back up again. He clung on to Beert, his face buried in his down. Eventually, though, Beert leveled off and the beating of his wings settled into a steady rhythm. Malcolm ventured a peep.

Crumblity crumb! The moon. It hung in the sky larger than the school's clock face. And . . . "What are those lights in the sky?"

Beert ducked. "What? Where? Sometimes you have to watch out for fireworks. Or a lantern. Although not much in winter."

"That sprinkle of lights." Malcolm turned his head. "They're everywhere!"

Beert looked again. "Stars above, Malcolm, you mean the stars above! You've heard of stars, haven't you?"

Malcolm had heard of stars, but nothing he had ever been told could prepare him for this. They spread across the sky like jelly on a piece of bread. Malcolm felt like he could look at them forever and never know them. Crumb, the Inside critters did have their pluses, but there were things out here that Malcolm couldn't even imagine.

Like the air. Earlier, on the roof, it had been fresh and cold, but now it was tinged with frost . . . and—he inhaled deeply—*possibility*. Malcolm could feel it pulse through his body with each beat of Beert's wings. He wasn't sure he'd ever be able to go back to enjoying his tail-safe exercise wheel after this.

Below him, a river glittered in the moon- and starlight. And across it, a building sprawled on its banks. As Beert flew closer, Malcolm could see that the building stretched for blocks and blocks, with walkways and tunnels connecting the parts of it.

"What is that?" Malcolm yelled to Beert.

Beert called over his wing, "Where we're going. It's a deserted tire factory. Closed up way back." He swooped, circled around, and landed on a rickety fire escape at the top floor. "And this is Building Five, Door Seventeen." He held out a wing. "Current headquarters of the Striped Shadow."

"We're here already?" Malcolm climbed off and stepped onto the rusty metal grid of the fire escape. He glimpsed the white of the snow on the ground far, far below. He was pretty sure he could fit through those gaps on the landing. He gulped and looked up at Beert instead — and froze.

On the wall, next to the battered door, there was a Mark. But how could there be a Mark out here? Still, Malcolm was sure of it. It looked like a two-pronged fork, stuck upside down in a plate of food.

Beert followed Malcolm's stare, swiveling his head around to the wall. "What — *that?* That's a Shadow Sign," he said. "It's how I knew where to go. The Striped Shadow uses these Signs —"

"But it's a Mark!" Malcolm interrupted. "*We* use these signs. The Midnight Academy does — inside the school."

"Really? But this is quite old. I know my mother taught me about Shadow Signs."

"I don't know this one, though." Malcolm tried to memorize its shape so he could recreate it back at McKenna. What did it mean, that Academy Marks were outside the school? Did Aggy know this?

"Well, in the Outside world, this means 'this is the place,'" Beert said.

Then he turned away from the Mark/Sign. "Malcolm, you should know: I'm not going in with you. I'll only be . . . you do better than me in enclosed spaces. But" — he ruffled Malcolm's fur with his beak — "be careful." He lowered his voice to a whisper. "The Striped Shadow is an

96

omni.[1] Omnis are unpredictable: they'll eat anything. I'm not saying he *will* eat you—I've never heard of him eating someone who's gone to him for help—but you can't fully trust an omni. They have no loyalty, not even to their own kind."

Malcolm nodded. He swallowed hard. "Okay." Then he gave a half smile. "Rats are omnis too, you know."

"I just want you to be aware of what you're getting into."

"Thanks," said Malcolm, and he turned again toward the door. "Do I knock?" He tapped at the door with the tip of his tail. How would anyone hear a tiny rat knocking in a building this big?

Then he spied it—at the bottom of the door, where it was dented the most: a gap. An entrance. Malcolm took a deep breath. "Meet you back here in a few minutes?"

Beert nodded. "I'll do some holding patterns out here to keep an eye on things. Just squeak when you're ready. I'll hear."

Malcolm nodded. He took another breath and slipped in through the space.

On the other side, he waited for his eyes to adjust. "Hello?" he called out. There was no answer.

Slowly, Malcolm came to realize he was in a vast room —the biggest space he had ever seen, bigger than the auditorium at McKenna, even. And it was full. Mountains—

---

[1] Omni = omnivore. An animal that eats both plants and meat—like humans.

rows upon rows upon rows of mountains of . . . junk. As Malcolm moved through the space, a multitude of scents —peanut butter, old motor oil, metal, burnt wood, acorns —stirred his nose. After several minutes, he reached the back of the room. This side had a huge bank of greasy windows through which the moon and starlight[2] barely penetrated. In their dim light, Malcolm could make out pieces of machinery as big as playground equipment.

Malcolm's ears twitched. Was that . . . breathing? A critter moving in the darkness? Every ratty instinct in him told him to stay in the shadows, to stay on the edges, but that was not why he was here.

"Hello," Malcolm called out again. The creature froze and slowly turned toward Malcolm. He was big, bigger than a cat but smaller than a dog (at least the dogs that walked by McKenna's windows during the day), with rough gray fur and strange markings on his face that made him look like he was wearing a mask.[3] The critter held his right front leg curled up under his chest.

For a brief second, Malcolm thought he saw the gleam of bared white teeth, but then the critter managed a tight smile instead. "Here to see the Striped Shadow, are you?"

Malcolm nodded.

---

[2] Because Malcolm wasn't ever going to forget about those stars. Even if he couldn't see them, he'd Know they were up there.

[3] Do you recognize what kind of critter this was? Malcolm didn't know at the time, but Beert and Honey Bunny told him all about raccoons later.

"Well, you'll have to come back. Tuesdays are for walk-ins. The rest of the week is by appointment only."

"But—I—" Malcolm started. He called after the quickly disappearing striped tail. "Wait!"

The critter turned and blinked, his eyes disappearing in the black of his mask. "Let me guess," he said. "It's an emergency, you may not be able to come back, and time is of the essence."

"Well . . . yeah," Malcolm said. "Pretty much."

The critter sighed. "Okay, I'll let him know. Wait here." He limped off, and Malcolm thought he heard him mutter, "Never give any notice, just think they can show up . . ." before he disappeared behind the heart of the pile of junk, a tower of—coat hangers?—so rusted, they had melded together.

Malcolm waited for what seemed like hours. He wondered if Beert was getting worried, or Honey Bunny too, for that matter. He sniffed a pile of tin cans. Embarrassingly, his stomach growled. How could he be hungry at a time like this?

He could hear voices behind the mountains, but he couldn't make out what they were saying. Then rattling plastic. Then silence. A long silence. Malcolm sniffed at a can near his foot. These didn't seem as old as some of the other stuff. Was that tuna? He snuffled closer.

Behind him, the masked critter cleared his throat.

Malcolm jumped, caught his right foot in a can, tripped,

and plowed into another, and suddenly the whole pile tumbled down around him in the loudest, longest noise he had ever heard. Seriously, no fifth-grader had anything on this racket. In fact, they could probably hear it back at McKenna.

"Oh, scrap," he said, when the cans finally stopped rolling around.

A can wobbled slowly to a rest near the curled front leg of the masked critter, and Malcolm saw the paw was missing. The animal cleared his throat. "Follow me."

It took all of Malcolm's willpower to get up and follow that critter. First of all, it was hard going, wading through all those spilled tin cans. Second, his paws quaked. But with each step, he thought of McKenna and the Academy and the legend of Ernie Bowman. He had to find out. It's what kept him going. Have you ever experienced that, Mr. Binney? Terrified to do something, yet it's also something you want more than anything else in the world?

The critter led him on a winding path, through the tunnels and amid piles to another wall, where a weathered tarp hung across two stacks of boxes, making deeper shadows in the darkness, if that was even possible.

The masked critter nodded. "Go on."

Malcolm took a step forward. Then he glanced back. His masked escort had disappeared. "Where did he go?"

The tarp rattled, and now Malcolm could see there was an animal under it, but only part of his striped tail curved out of the blackness. The Striped Shadow. Literally. He answered, "Acer runs errands for me. He's off on another one. Surely your question doesn't depend on him?" His voice was a deep, dramatic whisper that Malcolm had to strain to hear.

"Well, no," Malcolm admitted. But he would have liked to have another somewhat-friendly face with him. Or another face of any kind, for that matter. As a witness — in case any omnivore-ish snacking happened. Instead, Malcolm sidled toward the entrance, so he couldn't be trapped. "I heard that you help." Suddenly, Malcolm remembered his Academy training. Dignity and decorum, right? He stood up straight and cleared his throat. "I'm here tonight rep-

resenting the Midnight Academy of McKenna School . . . um, the big building on the other side of the river. We are in trouble. You see—"

"Please." The Striped Shadow swished his tail impatiently. "Don't waste my time. Skip the story. What do you want? A new home? Medical services? A troublesome mate relocated?"

Gristle, when this was all over, Malcolm was going to suggest to the Midnight Academy that they update their handbook. Dignity and decorum really didn't go very far these days. "Oh. Um . . . I guess we need information."

There was a pause. The tarp crinkled as the critter sat up. "Information?" he said. *"Information?"*

"Yes."

The tip of his tail flicked. It was white-tipped too, like Snip's had been, Malcolm noticed.

"Hmmm."

Malcolm tried to wait him out for an answer. He didn't want to be a pest. But the longer the silence stretched out, the more he felt the urge to nibble his whiskers.

Finally, the Striped Shadow spoke. "The truth is, you have an unusual request. I get asked for *things*, for *actions*, but not for information. You see, information is what I deal in. If I told everyone where I get the things I do—how I do the things I do—then why would anyone need me?"

Malcolm didn't know how to answer that.

The white tip of the Striped Shadow's tail twirled in a

slow circle. "Have you ever heard of a promise made under the stars?"

Malcolm twisted his own tail. "Um, no. In fact, I only saw stars for the first time to—"

"A promise made under the stars," the Striped Shadow interrupted, "is an Outside promise. A promise made in front of the whole wide world. When I help critters, they give me a promise—a promise made under the stars—to repay me. If I help you, are you willing to agree to this?"

Malcolm's feet had begun sweating. "I . . . I guess it depends on what it is I'm promising."

There was a low chuckle. "You're a smart one. Most critters have already agreed by now. But don't worry. It's not your first litter of pups or anything. It's only doing me a favor or giving me some information in return. See, that's really the heart of my business. I trade secrets and information. You need something. I give it to you, and in return you tell me or show me something that another client might need. Sometimes what you have is something I don't have a use for immediately, so I store it away for when I do. It's a wonderful business model, really. Low overhead."

A huge sense of relief washed over Malcolm. That was it? Why, he didn't have any secrets! Not any that would matter, anyway. What could the Striped Shadow possibly ask for? To reveal the big secret that Malcolm still sometimes snuck into the dumpster outside the cafeteria at night? He had no secrets. He had no information of importance.

"So, do you promise?"

"You don't even know what I want yet," Malcolm pointed out. "How do I know you can help me?"

"Fair enough," said the Striped Shadow. "Why don't you tell me."

Malcolm took a deep breath, and for the third time that night, he told about the school closing and the legend of Ernie Bowman (hopefully, *his* version wasn't changing!) and the Loaded Stash. He even threw in the fact that the Midnight Academy and the Striped Shadow were apparently using the same symbols, only calling them something different. "Do you think you can help?" Malcolm asked. "Do you know about any of that?"

The Striped Shadow was quiet again. A crinkle of tarp, and Malcolm caught a flash of an eye. It was masked too. "No. Not off the top of my whiskers. But . . . I have some sources I'd like to talk to. So how about this: Let's meet in a week, in the oaks outside your school, when that noise-maker on your roof clangs twelve. If I bring you information, you keep your promise. If I do not, you are not obligated to fulfill it."

That seemed fair. But . . . "How do I know which tree? And—a week! We don't have that kind of time—"

The Striped Shadow held up his tail. "If you want your information, meet me in a week." He pulled his tail back into the darkness of the tarp. "As for which tree . . . just look for a Shadow Sign."

CHAPTER 13
BLUE

A week. A week is a long time to wait. Especially if you're afflicted with hero brain. And especially when things aren't going so great.

Even though the Midnight Academy kept their regular Thursday-night meeting, they were clearly floundering. Honey Bunny and Malcolm had agreed that there was no point in bringing up the Striped Shadow unless, or until, he actually had something to tell them, so all that came out of the Midnight Academy meeting were stray bits and pieces. Malcolm shared the Shadow Sign/Mark with Aggy (saying he had found it "outside," with a vague wave of his paw). Aggy had found it interesting, but it didn't really change anything.

The most exciting thing was that Harriet had dragged in a yellowed scrap of paper that turned out to be a newspaper article from 1952 about Walton McKenna's death. There was one paragraph that had the critters leaning in: "Mr. McKenna, truly an outstanding gentleman, left a long and lasting impact on our community. Even in death, his concern was for the young people and the beauty of Clearwater. His will left all of his remaining money to the Clearwater Education Foundation and the Council for the Arts. Ironically, when it came time to disperse the funds, his bank accounts were empty. 'Generous to a fault, I guess,' his daughter Evelyn said with a laugh. 'That's just like Daddy, to give it all away before he could give it all away. He never did like banks, anyway.'"

"That's weird," said Tank. "Why say you're going to leave something for someone if you have nothing to give them? How did he have money to build all these things in our town, anyway?"

Jesse had jumped up at that. "Do you think they couldn't find his money because he stashed it in the school? In a Loaded Stash? Do ya? Do ya? Do ya?" He bounced with each question.

"Calm down," barked Honey Bunny. "I doubt it. He probably just spent it all."

"Most people think he was tricked out of it, or that it was stolen," Harriet said. "Possibly invested badly. But . . . maybe not."

"Well, even if any of that is true, there's nothing in there to help us *find* it," Polly pointed out.

And she was right. So the Academy was back to watching, listening, sniffing, exploring . . . and hoping.

The All-Stars weren't doing much better either. They had learned the Council Oak was right outside the school. An enormous oak tree that shadowed the auditorium. But the ground under it was too frozen to search for anything.

And despite Amelia making them stay in for a couple recesses to look at the yearbooks, they didn't have a whole lot more. They did find out that there used to be a pet blue jay in the library. The yearbook from 1939 included a picture of it perched near the windows. "Cute!" Kiera cried out. She read, "'This year brought a new mascot to the Clearwater Central High School library—an injured blue

jay. Mr. Randall Carson, Clearwater's handyman extraordinaire, rescued the bird, but when it became apparent that it would never fly again, he brought it to Miss Wilson in the library. "Blue's great company," Miss Wilson says. "I can't imagine the library without him now." ' "

"Huh," said Jovahn. "And now we're the McKenna Blue Jays. I wonder if that's why?"

For a minute, as Malcolm examined the picture, his hopes perked up. Could this be the "birds coming back to life" part of the story? But then again, like McKenna's missing money, even if it was, it didn't really help them in any way.

And McKenna's portrait was nowhere to be found. "For the last time, I don't know," Ms. Brumble grumbled. "I've never seen it. It's been gone since I started here."

Malcolm had even checked for it himself one night— the closest he came was finding a dark rectangle on the rear wall of the auditorium. You could tell a picture had hung there for a long, long time, the paint fading around it. But it was definitely gone now.

So they were left with the yearbooks.[1] Amelia paged through them, scanning pictures, while Kiera and Jovahn put together a slide-show presentation of current photos of the school. They hadn't exactly found a job for Skylar

---

[1] Amelia had nearly fainted when she realized she hadn't checked the yearbooks out from the library because of the yowling. She made Jovahn go down at recess time with her to fix it.

yet—mostly they were hoping that he wouldn't destroy anything.

It was like Sylvia's acorns. The Midnight Academy, the All-Stars, *everyone*, was just nibbling and gnawing. Getting the taste in their mouths, but what they really needed was someone—something—to crack the whole thing open. As each day passed, Malcolm's hopes hung more and more on the possibility of the Striped Shadow being the one to help them.

Then on Friday, after a disheartening Midnight Academy meeting the night before, Skylar stumbled into Room 11, lugging a black contraption that looked a little like a cross between a trombone and a weed whacker.[2]

"Well . . . hello there, Skylar," you said, as he walked past you. "Is that a . . . metal detector?" Skylar turned, and you winced as the disk part of it rammed, then tangled, into the legs of Jenna's chair.

Skylar nodded, wrestling to pull it free. "Amelia said we needed to find the time capsule under the oak tree. That we needed something sappy for the listening session."

Amelia sat up. "No, I didn't. I said—oh, never mind."

---

[2] Malcolm happened to know what both of these things were thanks to (1) frequent visits to Mrs. Findlay's music class (via Amelia's hood) and (2) a rather unfortunate science fair project that Michael brought in. That patch of hair grew back nicely, didn't it?

Skylar continued, "The ground may be frozen, and we can't dig down very far—digging is my hobby, you know—but we could still look for it. I found my metal detector under my bed, and my Gram was giving me a ride to school, so"—he brandished it, and Jenna ducked to avoid getting hit—"here it is."

Your mouth flapped a little. No offense, Mr. Binney, but Malcolm had noticed something peculiar going on ever since Skylar had joined your All-Stars group to save McKenna: no one was sure where he fit in anymore. He was like candied beets on a cafeteria tray. Technically, they're a vegetable. They belong in that compartment. But they're also sweet, so possibly they go better with the fruit? Or maybe even with dessert because they're "candied"?[3] And so you end up standing there in line with the serving spoon hanging over your tray while you try to figure out where to put them. *That* was the class staring at Skylar right now.

Jovahn jumped in. "That is so cool, Skylar! You are a genius. *Genius.*" (Well, maybe everyone except Jovahn didn't know what to think of Skylar.) He turned to you. "Can we look, Mr. Binney? Can we go check under the trees? Can we go now?" He was already half out of his seat.

You finally closed your mouth. You pointed at the window. "It's raining."

And it was. Pouring, in fact, in that freezing-cold,

---

[3] For what it's worth, candied beets are a mistake wherever you put them. Skylar, however, had potential.

almost-as-much-ice-as-water, first-hint-of-spring rain. The playground was going to be a mess later.

"Please?" Jovahn said it so eagerly, Malcolm was pretty sure you didn't have the heart to turn him down.

You sighed. "Maybe right before lunch."

It was still raining then, but that didn't stop the class from trudging out to the giant oak tree on the edge of the McKenna school property. As you hunched, water dripping down your face, your hands red with cold, you looked a little like you'd rather be in the dry teachers' lounge with Ms. Brumble. But Malcolm couldn't be sure.

Of course, you turned it into a lesson, Mr. Binney. "The reason this tree is called the 'Council Oak' is because Native Americans and other travelers used it as a meeting place. You can see that because of its size and location along the river, it'd be easy to spot. Years ago, it was struck by lightning; that's why it's got this funny V shape now."

Meeting place? Oak tree? Malcolm's ears perked up. Amelia actually had her jacket's hood up today, so Malcolm had to brave the elements in her coat pocket for this outing. The only way to see was to stick his head out into the rain, and, gristle, rain definitely fell into the negative category for Outside critters.

You continued, "Because of the history, I'm not surprised if they chose to bury a time capsule here. Well, Skylar, let's fire it up."

But despite pass after pass, there was no blip of anything the size or shape of a time capsule.

"Are you sure this thing works?" Kiera grumped. Her hair frizzed out from under her hood. She also looked like she'd rather be inside.

But it *was* working, because they did uncover a few treasures: twelve bottle caps, a button, four nails, and two nickels. But no time capsule.

The bell rang. "Time to head in, folks," you said. "I'm sorry, All-Stars, but there's nothing here. Maybe the time capsule has already been dug up."

They plodded back in. "Are you going to cry?" Kiera asked Amelia.

"No." Amelia scowled. But Kiera was right; Amelia's face wore a pinched look that Malcolm didn't recognize. He wasn't even surprised when she ducked into the girls' bathroom instead of heading to lunch later. Once they got into the stall, she pulled her feet up on the bench and held Malcolm close to her. After a minute, he realized that the shaking of her shoulders meant she *was* crying.

Malcolm didn't know what to do. He wanted to get down, use his notebook, and ask her what was going on, but he couldn't leave her. So he nuzzled her face the best he could and hoped she'd talk soon.

She didn't get the chance to, though. Right about then, voices could be heard in the hall. "I told you, I know where she is. She's been hiding out in here for weeks."

The door pounded open. "Amelia?" Kiera's voice rang out. Malcolm's and Amelia's eyes met. Amelia sat up fast, wiped her face, and pulled her feet up higher on the bench so they couldn't be seen under the door.

"Shhh! You can't yell," whispered another voice. "Do you want every teacher to know we're out here?"

Jovahn?! Amelia mouthed to Malcolm. He was as startled as she was.

"What are you doing?" Kiera said with a little shriek. "You can't be in here! This is the girls' room!"

"Oh, please," Jovahn muttered. "A toilet's a toilet."

Then a knock on their stall door. "Amelia?" Jovahn called out softly. With another swipe at her eyes, Amelia slowly extended one leg, then the other. She stood and unlocked the door.

Jovahn was on the other side. Kiera leaned around behind him, and Skylar stood gaping in the background, still propping the hallway door open. Jovahn waved for him to shut it.

"What are you doing here?" Amelia asked.

"Looking for you," Skylar said.

"What's going on?" Jovahn asked with a frown, glancing around. "Where is your lunch?"

Amelia paused like she might say something, and then she shook her head. "I don't want to talk about it."

"You're not supposed to be in here, you know. You're supposed to go to the cafeteria, then straight outside,"

Kiera said, her arms crossed. "I told Jovahn—" Jovahn stepped on her foot and she paused. She yanked it out and glared at him.

"Is it because of the time capsule?" he asked. "Because Skylar says that just because we didn't find anything doesn't mean it isn't out there. Maybe it's not metal."

Amelia shook her head. "No, not exactly. Although I did really want to find it. It just seems like . . . Do you ever feel like you have no control over anything? They decide they want to close our school—and *poof*, they can. And then . . ." Malcolm watched her closely. What was behind that "and then"? But Amelia didn't finish. She just drooped.

Kiera was watching too. Slowly, she uncrossed her arms. Then she did the most surprising thing Malcolm had ever seen her do—and he had seen her bring in an entire lunch consisting of only blue food.

She held out her hand to Amelia.

"Come on," she said, pulling Amelia out of the stall. "We finished the slide show, we think. But we need you to proofread it. And one of those nickels we found outside is super freaky—it's from 1938 and has a guinea pig carved into it! Mr. Binney says it's a bobo nickel or something."

Malcolm stared up at Kiera as she led the group out of the bathroom. Maybe Kiera's water dish was deeper than it seemed.

CHAPTER 14

THE COUNCIL OAK

Then finally, *finally*, it was Wednesday again and the night
Malcolm was due to meet with the Striped Shadow. He
had had a week to think about how he'd get back outside,
and he had come to the conclusion that it'd be easiest to
sneak out through Sylvia's nest. Honey Bunny had reluc-
tantly agreed, even though it meant Malcolm had to go
alone.

"Sylvia?" he whispered. He didn't want to wake up her
squirrelings *or* surprise her. He figured either one might
result in him getting bitten.

"She's out," a squirreling said, poking his head out of
their nest.

"Hey, it's that bat, Malcolm," his sibling said, popping up next to him. "Did you bring corn dogs?"

"*Rat*," Malcolm corrected. "And you heard that? I thought you were sleeping last time."

The squirrelings shrugged. "Squirrels have good hearing."

Malcolm tiptoed around them. "I don't really need your mom; I'm just passing through tonight."

The squirrelings bobbed in the nest and waved. "Okay —we'll tell her you stopped by."

That was weird—Sylvia being out. Where would a squirrel go in the middle of the night? Squirrels, from what Malcolm understood, were day critters. And Sylvia had been so concerned about the Dangers Outside.

But Malcolm didn't have time to contemplate it further. He was worried he might have missed the clock chiming. Maybe the Striped Shadow was already there, waiting for him. He struck Malcolm as a critter who wouldn't hang around long if someone didn't show.

Malcolm pushed through the loose bricks and immediately was blasted by frigid air. The light flickered from dark to darker and back again as clouds whisked by the moon. The oak trees' branches clacked against one another in the wind. The stars were nowhere to be seen. Across the parking lot, the Council Oak swayed, taller than the rest. You were right, Mr. Binney: it was a funny shape. It must have once been a majestic tree, but now it looked like someone had snipped out a pie piece from the tallest part of it. Malcolm itched to get out there. He would bet the whole Loaded Stash that the Council Oak was Marked with a Shadow Sign.

Malcolm took a running start, then flung himself at the tree branches next to the roof. For a moment, he got the same soaring feeling he'd had when he flew with Beert the other night. Then, unlike with Beert, he started to fall.

Malcolm caught himself on the tiny tips of a branch. They were so slim, even Malcolm's small weight bent them down. He pulled himself up and crawled along the branch until he came to the trunk. Then he crossed to the other side of the tree. Here, it was easier. These branches crisscrossed with the next tree's. Malcolm hopscotched from tree to tree, until he was in the branches of the tallest of them all: the Council Oak. Crumb, if this Council Oak was big from the ground, those nutters ought to see it from its branches! It was like a whole world up here. Malcolm made his way to the center of the V of the tree. Was that . . . ? By crumb! Another Mark. The same "dwell here" Mark that was on the dictionary in the library. Malcolm wondered if it was an Inside or an Outside critter who had carved it there.

"Nice jump," said a deep whisper from behind Malcolm, which nearly made him jump in a whole different way and fall out of the tree.

He whirled around. The Striped Shadow, in the branches above him. Malcolm could barely make him out.

"How was your week?" the Striped Shadow asked.

Malcolm opened his mouth, but suddenly the entirety of the week weighed on him. He didn't have the time or the energy to play games. So he answered with a question. "Did you find anything out?" Gristle, he sounded *tough*.

The Striped Shadow tilted his head, and his eyes flashed in his raccoon mask. "Maybe. Do we have a deal?"

"Really? You found something?" Malcolm stumbled over his words, the tough-guy voice already evaporating. After so many days of nothing turning up, of everything leading to *no*s and more *no*s, he was fully expecting the Striped Shadow to say the same thing.

The Shadow nodded. "Of course. It's what I do. It's why critters come to me. So, do we have a deal?"

Malcolm remembered about the promise under the stars. A secret or a favor. Now, after a week of nothing, it felt like he had even less to lose. "Yes, that's fine."

"Well, then. There are two bits of information you may find interesting. First, your 'Midnight Academy'—they're quite well known." He tilted his head again. "When I talked to one of the oldest critters around this school, she knew of them immediately. She also said that the Academy used to keep their records in a 'Marked' set of books. Inside the books, the Academy would underline certain words to make a message. It sounds rather primitive to me, but if you look for these Marked books, you may be able to fill in some of the gaps in your story."

Sweet niblets, that was *genius*, as Jovahn would say.

This must have been before computers. Malcolm felt like he should have been able to guess this, though. It was not that different from how he communicated with Amelia, only he pointed to the words with his tail instead of underlining them. "How do we know where the books are?" Malcolm asked. "I mean, I know you said they were Marked, but have you ever been in a school? Every room is packed with books. And there are dozens of rooms. You could spend weeks just in the library looking for Marks."

"Ah, but that's the other thing," the Shadow continued. "It seems that the Academy has not always been a critters-only club."

"What?"

"Years and years ago, before any of your current members were hatchlings, the Academy always had one human who helped them. Someone they trusted, who kept their secrets and served as a bridge to the human world. I don't know all that you do, but I can imagine that sometimes it's hard to carry out your work, simply because you're critters among humans. Anyway, this person also guarded the Marked books of Academy records and made sure they were passed to the next generation of pets."

"Ernie Bowman!" Malcolm whispered. It had to be. It all made sense.

"Maybe, but my source didn't know that name. But this group of human helpers did call themselves something: 'the Elastic Order of Suspenders.'"

"Suspenders?" Malcolm remembered the old catalog page in the Dictionary Niche. "That fits with our legend, doesn't it?"

The Striped Shadow nodded. "It does seem to suggest there is something to your story."

"And now," Malcolm said, "we need to find the Marked books, and we can learn the rest of it. Do you think there's still someone who is in the Elastic Order of Suspenders in our building who could show us the books?"

"My source didn't think so," the Striped Shadow said. "She hadn't heard anything about it since she was a kitten. That was before any of the current teachers were there. But the last one was a 'librarian,' whatever that is. My source said that'd mean something to an Inside critter."

But Malcolm had stopped listening: his brain had snagged on an earlier word. A word that had shut down all his senses. His tongue felt like a waterlogged football. "D-d-did you say 'kitten'?"

The Striped Shadow smirked slightly. "Yes." Was Malcolm imagining it, or had the raccoon's eyes flicked to something behind him for a second? "I don't normally divulge my sources like this. In my business, it works much better to keep all the business partners separate. But this case was quite unusual." He dropped to Malcolm's branch. At the same time, Malcolm stepped behind the trunk of the tree. The Striped Shadow followed. "I think I told you the other night that I deal in secrets and favors. It's all about being a good listener, really. Noticing things.

Then you put them together. All these so-called problems of critters are actually interconnected. Like a web.

"For example, this winter I was approached by a critter who needed something. I asked her what she could help me with, and she said she knew secrets, so many secrets, of a school she had hidden in for years. I scoffed at first —because why would I bother with Inside business? I had enough on the Outside. But she recognized my Shadow Signs. That intrigued me. So I struck a deal with her. And I tucked her secrets away for later. And then, last week you came along. You also knew my Shadow Signs. And you needed something."

No, it couldn't be. Malcolm trembled, his heart thudding. He glanced left and right. Where to go? He had walked to the end of a branch. He whirled and sprang across to another tree.

The Striped Shadow, however, continued talking as if nothing had happened. "Suddenly, I had a use for her secrets. And I had a way to give her what she wanted. It's business, you see, Malcolm."

A cloud scuttled in front of the moon, and in that blink of darkness, the Striped Shadow leaped across to Malcolm's tree. The branches bowed low under his weight, swinging wildly, and Malcolm was almost thrown off. As the raccoon jumped, for a second Malcolm thought he spied something funny with his front paw, and then the Shadow was there, breathing in Malcolm's face, too close for him to see anything but the pointed teeth that were now bared.

"Remember your deal, Malcolm. Because, as it turns out, I believe you can help this critter in return."

The Striped Shadow twitched his white-tipped tail as if he was signaling something—or somebody. "I'd like you to meet someone, Malcolm. I believe you may have already met. Still, allow me to introduce . . . Blackberry."

Malcolm had been creeping backwards again. He was almost to the trunk of this tree. Now he spun around to run. He wasn't even sure in what direction. Up or down. To jump if he needed to. It didn't matter. He had to get away, get Inside. *Now.* Sylvia was right: there were Dangers in these trees.

But there was nowhere to go—because behind him was a cat. A black cat with overlong claws, spider breath, and a white-tipped tail. A cat who was supposed to be drowned, dead, by Malcolm's own actions. A cat very much alive and—if not well—at least *here* and licking her whiskers. A cat once named Blackberry as a kitten, but who more recently went by another name.

Snip.

Malcolm felt his legs go out. And then he fell right out of that tree.

CHAPTER 15
THE DEAL

It turns out that falling is not at all like flying. For one, you're not in control. As Malcolm fell, he bounced off of branches, and twigs scraped at his ears. And then there's the landing. The landing is much, much worse when you're falling. He hit a melting snowbank hard, and everything went dark.

When Malcolm woke up, he wasn't sure where he was. Cheez, he had been having the worst dream! Snip—looming over him!

Then Malcolm opened his eyes. Snip—looming over him! And the whole night came rushing back. The meeting with the Striped Shadow. The promise under the stars. And Snip. Alive.

"You again!" she hissed, her voice just as raspy-dry as it had been in Malcolm's nightmares. "It's always *you*—always in the way of what I want."

He leaped to his feet, backing away quickly until he ran into the tree trunk again. He scampered up it and hid behind a dried clump of oak leaves. "How . . . how . . . You were dead! Honey Bunny told me. The lankies found something." He didn't know if it was from his fall or from seeing his nightmares come to life, but Malcolm felt wobbly, like the whole world was tilting and if he didn't hang on tight, he could slide right off.

"I don't know what they found," she said, pacing back and forth below him. "But it wasn't me. Could be the lankies weren't telling the truth. Could be your Academy wasn't." Malcolm saw that, while still thin, Snip was actually looking healthier than the last time he had seen her —scary-skinny and soaking wet in the boiler room of the school. If you looked closely, you could still see a bare white line where her too-tight collar[1] had once been, but mostly her fur had now grown over it.

The Striped Shadow stirred under a shrub. Apparently, everyone had come down from the Council Oak. Malcolm wondered how long he had been out. His eyes pinged between the two critters beneath him. "How do you two even know each other?"

----

[1] The collar had been put on her as a kitten, but then when she had been lost (or forgotten, depending on who you asked), she had grown and it hadn't. Malcolm had been the one to gnaw it off her.

"Like I said," the Shadow answered, "she approached me. Much like you did—only without knocking over two thousand tin cans and waking up the whole neighborhood. And she knew things. About the school. About the Inside. It's been very valuable for my business. But I still owe her the one thing *she* wants. And I think *you* can provide it." He gestured with a paw at the dark bulk of McKenna. "Entrance back into McKenna. Let Blackberry in, and we'll be even."

"Are you crazy?!" Malcolm nearly shouted. "She's demented. She's evil. She . . . can't be trusted. She flung me out a window, she slashed my ear, she made my friend fall off the clock tower—"

Snip calmly blinked. "Says who?" Her tail with the white tip started weaving in a figure eight. Malcolm stared at it for a second, then pulled his eyes away. Oh, no, he was not going to get sucked into that hypnotic trick of hers again.

"I do!"

The Striped Shadow's tail bristled under the bush. "Malcolm, you agreed—"

"She *ate* Beert's owlets, she kidnapped our Academy leader . . . she was going to mix this crazy brew into the nutters' water! And all because of a mistake! She thought she had been abandoned, but she even had *that* messed up. All of that—for the wrong reasons! Who does that?"

Snip's tail lowered. Her yellow eyes, so intently staring at Malcolm, blinked away.

The Striped Shadow said quietly, "So you are saying she doesn't deserve anything."

"Yes!" Finally the Shadow understood!

But the raccoon shook his head. "No, that's not the way it works, Malcolm. You don't get to decide who to help or how to help or even to judge what kind of help they're asking for. First of all, who are *you* to decide any of that?"

Malcolm squirmed. Hadn't he heard this before? Then he remembered, *he* had said it, with Billy and Jesse, when he first met Sylvia. But that was different! Sylvia was a helpless squirrel—with squirrelings, no less!—not a murderous carnivore with fish-hook claws.

The Striped Shadow continued, "But secondly—and mostly, as far as I'm concerned—you *promised*. Under the stars. You don't want to break an under-the-stars promise."

Malcolm didn't care. He couldn't *keep* an under-the-stars promise either—not if this was what it meant. "You said I'd need to tell you a secret. I'm ready to do that. But I can't do this—I won't. I'm not going to put everyone I know at risk."

Snip snarled then. "Forget it. I'll find my own way. I don't need anything from him. As for you"—she arched her back and her fur spiked in the Shadow's direction—"I should have known not to trust someone who hides in the shadows." She dragged her claws along the ground, leaving long scrapes in the frozen dirt and snow, then stalked off.

"Good! Leave!" Malcolm shouted after her. "Keep away from our school!"

Behind him, the Striped Shadow blinked once. Twice. "I have to say, Malcolm, I'm a bit appalled at your manners. Is this how you do things Inside? Make promises, then break them?" He slipped through the bushes next to the parking lot. "This isn't over. Don't think I won't be back. It's bad business if I don't collect on a deal. So it never—*ever*—happens." And with that, he plunged into the brush. It rattled as he made his way down the slope to the river.

Malcolm took a few steadying breaths, then crawled back up to the top of the Council Oak. Oh, gristle! What had he done? He traced the Mark with his paw. He didn't feel right about breaking his promise, but no matter how many times he replayed the situation in his mind, he couldn't figure out what else he could have done. Let Snip back into McKenna? There was no way. Maybe this was what Jesse and Billy meant when they said Outside and Inside critters didn't mix.

And what should Malcolm do now? The information that the Striped Shadow had shared pointed the Midnight Academy in a real direction for the first time. And what had the Shadow said—that the last Elastic Order of Suspenders member had been a librarian? The Marked books must be in the library! Maybe. Hopefully. Or this all could be another dead end.

Malcolm slumped against the tree trunk. He knew he

should go in and tell Honey Bunny what he had learned. The rabbit had probably eaten a pound of banana chips by now, worrying about him. And there really was no time to waste—the school board listening session was coming up fast. If they were going to get to the bottom of this Loaded Stash business, every minute counted.

But while Malcolm himself was eager to start scanning books for Marks, he couldn't stand the thought of talking to Jesse or Billy or Honey Bunny or anyone in the Academy who had reassured him over the last few months that Snip could not possibly still be around. Would they even believe him now? Or would they think he was *still* imagining things?

Or maybe—worst of all—maybe they had known all along that Snip *was* alive, and they had lied about it to make Malcolm feel better.

Either way, Malcolm wasn't ready to face them yet.

CHAPTER 16
AMELIA'S NOTE

It was later than Malcolm thought when he got back inside
—there was no time to visit the library to look for Marked
books. Malcolm gave Honey Bunny a quick wave from the
hall to show that, indeed, nothing had swooped down and
eaten him, and then he had to dash to the Comf-E-Cube
before the morning custodian started making his rounds.
Malcolm was more than a little relieved to not have to explain what had happened in the oak.

And then, that next day, the unthinkable happened.
Something so rare, so unbelievable, that even Malcolm's
quandary[1] from the night before fell right out of his head.

---

[1] Quandary = dilemma, problematic situation. Vocabulary from 2/22. Normally,
Malcolm's biggest quandary was which to eat first: Jovahn's Pop-Tarts or
Amelia's graham crackers. Crumb, did he long for those simpler days.

The bell rang to start the school day, and Amelia was
. . . *late*.

"Maybe she's absent." Jovahn stared at the door as
he offered a piece of his Pop-Tart to Malcolm. Malcolm
reached for it, but it was way over his head. He squeaked,
and Jovahn adjusted the Pop-Tart range. "Sorry," he said,
frowning and jiggling his leg.

You came in then, Mr. Binney. "Okay, everyone. Settle
in. Math warm-ups on the board."

"See you, mousie," Jovahn said with a pat, then headed
back to his desk.

And then suddenly, Amelia *was* there, striding through
the classroom door, her head high, color-coded notebooks
clutched to her chest, eyes blinking bright.

And Malcolm's mouth fell open.

Amelia marched to the table she shared with him. She
sat down with a *thump*, then flipped open her math notebook so fast, she tore the page.

Malcolm stared.

Amelia had walked into the classroom *in her socks*. Not
as in, she was carrying her shoes and was about to put
them on. She was . . . *without her shoes*.

As you know, Mr. Binney, it's a rule at McKenna that if
you want to play in the snow — not just stay on the black-
top (where the puddles are) — you have to wear boots.
So kids did, and they often left their shoes accidentally at
home. It happened every day in Room 11.

But not to Amelia.

131

Amelia had never, not once, ever forgotten anything. Not a permission slip, or when it was Veterans Day, or her popcorn money, or even to completely clear her lunch tray before stacking it. She was the one who, year after year, teachers depended on to remind the class about fire drills and spelling quizzes.

And now, here she was: shoeless.

Even you paused at that, Mr. Binney. Meanwhile, the rest of the class turned and stared.

The phone rang. A waver of worry crinkled between your eyes, but you answered it.

It was more than a waver of worry for Malcolm. His stomach twisted, churning like the time he had eaten an apple-scented eraser, thinking it was an apple. As he watched Amelia's dark head, so intent on her math warm-up, so intent on not making eye contact with him, Malcolm knew something was horribly, horribly wrong.

Have you ever had a friend who wouldn't tell you everything, Mr. Binney? I remember that one time Jenna lied about having gum in her mouth, and then she played her recorder and it got stuck in there. So you know about lies and not saying all the truth. But that really isn't the same thing. There's nothing *personal* in it. When a friend won't tell you everything, well, it feels a little like you are waiting for a punch in the gut.

Malcolm raised his eyes to Jovahn in the next row over. He was watching Amelia too. "Hey," Jovahn whispered to her. He opened his mouth to say something, then bit his lip. "Did you see my jump on the playground?" he finally asked.

Amelia shook her head, without looking up.

Tianna, as usual, zeroed in on any whisper like she was a heat-seeking missile. She sniffed at Amelia. "Nice socks."

Amelia didn't answer. She did, however, blink very rapidly.

"Skylar?" you called from the front of the room, the phone still in your hand. "Are you supposed to be down in the resource room? And, Jovahn, get to work, please."

"Oh!" Skylar lurched up, knocking a stack of comic books and his box of sixty-four crayons (which weren't even supposed to be out) all over the floor.

You sighed and answered, "Yes, hold on. I'll send him."

Jovahn took advantage of this distraction. "What is it?" he whispered to Amelia. Malcolm echoed him, stretching his front paws up high on the cage wall and squeaking as loudly as he dared.

Amelia ignored them both. Her pencil hovered over her notebook, not moving.

"Amelia!" Jovahn said, kicking her desk a little. Malcolm squeaked again.

But Amelia didn't answer.

You finally hung up the phone, Mr. Binney. Skylar headed down the hall, and you started walking around the room, checking assignment notebooks. When you got to Amelia's (which was the only one in the room without a single creased or wrinkled page), Amelia finally moved.

She flipped to the front of it and pulled out a pink square sheet of paper. Without looking at you—do you remember, Mr. Binney?—she handed you a note.

Malcolm's nose twitched. What was this? He had seen notes before. Usually they were about how a student had to go to the dentist at 12:30, so please have them waiting in the lobby, or that it was a student's birthday on Friday —would it be okay to send cupcakes? But none of those caused apple-scented-eraser-like digestive problems.

You unfolded and scanned it. "Oh, Amelia. Really?" Your voice dropped, like you *had* been punched in the stomach. It scared Malcolm even further. Jovahn wasn't even pretending to write. He craned his neck to see the note. You folded it up. "Let's talk in the hall."

Amelia reached up and pulled the elastic out of her hair so it swung down like a curtain—or a shield. She padded out of the room after you in her socks.

The class was pin-drop quiet. (Jovahn actually has a pin for these situations, but he was so distracted right then that he forgot to get it out.) Anyway, you must have known that the class would be listening, Mr. Binney, because you closed the door.

After a few minutes, which seemed like hours, you both returned. You looked tired, Mr. Binney. And Amelia now had on a pair of spare sneakers that were way more scuffed than anything she would normally associate with. As she slipped back into her seat, you asked, "Do you want to say something, Amelia? Or I could."

Amelia finally glanced at Jovahn and Malcolm. Her eyes did that super-fast blinking again. She looked down at her notebook and cleared her throat.

"I'm moving. Next week."

Amelia moving.

Amelia leaving.

Amelia moving.

Amelia leaving.

For the rest of the morning, it was like Malcolm's brain was stuck on his tail-safe plastic exercise wheel, going around and around and never going anywhere. Nothing —not slightly pulverized cheese puffs offered by Skylar, or the power going out again and everyone having to push their desks over to the windows to see to do their math, or even Amelia reaching the ending of *Mrs. Frisby and the Rats of NIMH*—could get Malcolm's thoughts to stop circling. His midmorning naptime was spent chewing up a toilet paper tube.

After Amelia had made her announcement, Mr. Binney had talked for a while to the class about how they'd miss her, but how her new school would be a lot of fun too. Malcolm had actually gone a little weak and had to lie down in his shredded paper. At the time, he didn't exactly know what "moving" entailed, but he certainly understood what "last day" meant.

A few weeks earlier, the class had made valentines out

of construction paper. Malcolm felt exactly like the construction paper that ended up in the recycling bin. A discarded piece of paper, with the heart cut out.

Malcolm was so distraught that he almost unlatched his own cage and climbed out to sit on Amelia's shoulder —right in front of everyone. Because if Amelia was leaving, well, then, what did it matter? Malcolm would leave too. He could live in her hood, right?

The rest of the morning was a blur. The apple-scented-eraser lump in Malcolm's stomach grew. Malcolm noticed that Jovahn didn't eat his snack either.

At lunch recess, you let Amelia stay in to play with Malcolm, Mr. Binney. You brought her a sandwich, apple, and a milk. She let Malcolm out of his cage, but she still wouldn't meet his eyes. He nudged their notebook. When she opened it, Malcolm jumped from letter to letter. Only three. "WHY?"

Amelia took a deep breath and finally talked to him. "Oh, Malcolm. My dad lost his job in December. We can't afford to stay where we are anymore. We're moving in with my cousins."

There was a noise at the door. Both Malcolm and Amelia looked up. Jovahn stood in the doorway, scuffing his sneakers. "How come you didn't say?" he asked finally.

Amelia sighed and stroked Malcolm's back. "I guess I was hoping it wouldn't happen."

Jovahn walked closer. "Where are you going?"

"An apartment on the north side. I'll finish the year at Fairfax."

Jovahn kicked at the table leg. "It's not fair." He slumped in a chair. "There's got to be something we can do. What if we take up a class collection—would that be enough money?"

Amelia rolled her eyes. "Have you ever paid rent? It's, like, a lot."

"Well, what if we buy lottery tickets? It's worth a try."

Amelia smiled crookedly. "If you won the lottery, you'd give my parents the money?"

Jovahn considered. "Well, maybe. Yeah ... after I bought a car or two—a Lamborghini, of course. And have you seen those new Nike basketball shoes?"

As the two friends talked, Malcolm wondered: Why was everything about money for humans? Money was the reason McKenna might close. There wasn't enough money to fix the windows, to unflood the basement, to repair the wiring. And they talked about it all the time, too. "My mom forgot to give me lunch money today." "I need fifty-six more dollars before I can buy the next War Hero robot fighter." "You owe me two dollars or a packet of fruit gummy snacks." Even you, Mr. Binney—the night before, you and Ms. Brumble had been wondering if you should honeymoon in Door County to save money. It seemed like humans never had enough of it. They spent their time saving, earning, arguing, or complaining about it.

How could something Malcolm had never seen have such importance?

Finally, Jovahn and Amelia grew quiet and Malcolm entered the conversation. He spelled out "STAY."

Amelia scratched his ears. "Oh, Malcolm, believe me. I wish I could. But it turns out that nutters are a lot like critters, really. We have to go where the lankies tell us. Sometimes it doesn't matter how much you don't want to. Some things *are* insurmountable."

CHAPTER 17
KALE

That night, Malcolm listened to the sounds of Ms. Brumble cleaning up the school. The *swish* of her broom, the *bang-tap* of the dustpan, the *click* of the door shutting, the *squeak* of the wheels as she moved to the next room and did it all over again. Far off, Malcolm heard the clock chime eleven. Now it was the buzz of the school's security system and the *vroom* of your Honda in the parking lot, Mr. Binney, picking her up.

Finally, Malcolm rolled himself out of his Comf-E-Cube. He knew Honey Bunny was waiting, wondering how things had gone the night before with the Striped Shadow. He should probably go down to Honey Bunny's room before the Academy meeting. But Malcolm wasn't sure he could drag himself there. He didn't know what to say to Honey Bunny. First, Snip was *alive*. Had Honey Bunny lied? Or did he not know? But mostly, it was Amelia's news. It was too tender and fresh. Malcolm didn't think he could talk about it, yet it hurt so much, he wasn't sure he could speak about anything else.

So, in the end, instead of heading toward the second grade wing, Malcolm found himself heading to the library. Maybe a little browsing for Marked books would get the ache in his chest under control so that he could face Honey Bunny.

It had been a long time since Malcolm had been in the library alone. It was both darker and quieter than he remembered. He thought about getting the Academy flashlight, but he wasn't sure he was big enough to turn it on or carry it. And that was the last thing Malcolm needed —something else to feel lousy about.

So Malcolm wandered the aisles on his own. He started with what he thought was an obvious place—the shelf that held the Marked dictionary. But no other book there had any sort of Academy Markings,[1] not even the yearbooks. Huh. Malcolm had been so sure that was where to look that he didn't know where to go next. The library was gigantic. There was no way one rat could check all these

---

[1] There were plenty of other markings, however. Mostly, the usual: crayon, pen, pencil, but even some of the rare ones—sticker, whiteout, and one that Malcolm was pretty sure was grape juice.

books, not even a rat with a hero brain who wanted to do it all by himself.

The computer light flickered up front. "Maybe he's in here. Malcolm?"

He froze. "Aggy?"

"Yes—back here," Aggy called. And the next thing Malcolm knew, the iguana was coming around the corner and Honey Bunny hopped in front of her.

"Hey, I thought we were meeting, rat," the rabbit whispered before Aggy got there.

But Aggy pressed in. "Oh, Malcolm. We were so worried about you."

"We—*you* were?" Honey Bunny jerked his head toward Aggy.

"Yes." Aggy nodded. "I heard about your nutter."

And there it was. So much for hiding in the library! Malcolm felt like he had been hit in the face with a dodge ball. He sat down heavily on one of the library beanbags.

Honey Bunny glanced back and forth between the two critters. "What? I thought—" He turned to Malcolm. "Weren't we going to tell Aggy . . ."

"Amelia's moving," Malcolm blurted.

Honey Bunny flinched, then blew out a breath of air. "Oh." Then he shifted and stood. "Hey, you know, I just remembered something I've got to do back in the classroom. Malcolm, you want to meet me there when you're done here?" And without waiting for an answer, he pushed the library door open and hopped through it.

Aggy turned back to Malcolm. "When?"

"Next week." Malcolm couldn't bring himself to answer with more than two words.

She jerked her head toward the door. "You know, it's why he's so gruff all the time."

"What?" Malcolm thought they were talking about Amelia moving.

Aggy nodded toward the door. "Honey Bunny. HB. He had a special connection with a nutter like you and Amelia have. They doted on each other. I've never seen such a bond. And then one day, *poof!* The boy was gone. Just . . . moved, overnight. No goodbye, no warning, nothing. They never saw each other again. Now, ever since, Honey Bunny has put up a wall. Oh, he's loyal to the nutters and the school, but he doesn't let anyone grow close. It's too hard on him." She nudged Malcolm's ear. "This news about Amelia is shocking and sad, but you're lucky, you know. You've got a few more days to make more memories."

"Lucky?" Malcolm wheeled around. "We're supposed to be together forever!"

Aggy lifted her head and her orange golf-ball-size eyes crinkled in concern. "Forever? Oh, Malcolm. No. They all leave eventually. You know that, right?"

"What do you mean?"

She sighed. "Sometimes I forget that this is your first year in the Academy. You've done so much. This should have been in your pledge training. But you really didn't get all your training, did you?" She slipped her tail around Malcolm. "They leave, Malcolm. The nutters leave. All of them. The school year ends. And next fall . . . you'll have a new class of nutters."

Malcolm pulled away to stare at Aggy. He remembered those comments that had niggled at him. You had said it, Mr. Binney, after the disastrous music rehearsal: *"We have a long way to go before this bunch is ready to leave McKenna for middle school."* And Tianna, too. *"We're out of here anyway at the end of the school year."* Was this what everyone had been talking about? How did everyone know this, but Malcolm didn't? What else had he been missing?

"What? *All* of them?" It was bad enough that Amelia was leaving, but Jovahn, too? Malcolm would even miss being crammed in Skylar's pocket. "But . . . where do they go?"

"Summer vacation. It's like a really long weekend. They stay home for a couple of months. Then in the fall, your nutters will be sixth-graders. They move over to the middle school. You'll still have Mr. Binney," she said in a rush after catching a glimpse of Malcolm's face. "And you'll likely have a glorious summer in one of your nutters' homes before a new year and new nutters come to be fifth-graders."

Malcolm felt like he was falling through the wall all over again.

"I'm sure they'll come back to visit you. Many will never forget you — for their entire lives. But it's how things are,

Malcolm. Don't think of it as sad. Think of it as how there are more nutters to love every year. Maybe there will even be another Amelia."

Malcolm knew Aggy meant well, but this made the apple-scented-eraser ache start again in his belly. Another Amelia! What was she saying? He closed his eyes. He tried to imagine knowing other nutters the way he knew Amelia. And then losing them. Over and over again.

There was a long pause, and then Aggy said, "It's worse to not love them, Malcolm. To be there, but not be there." She squeezed her tail around him. "It's like when I first came to McKenna. My lanky always brought in butternut squash for me. Oh, how I loved butternut squash. But then one day, he replaced it with this strange, leafy stuff called kale. I turned up my snout at it for the longest time. Then I finally tried it. And guess what? Delicious."

What the crumb was Aggy talking about now? Butternut squash? Kale? For once in Malcolm's life, he couldn't imagine eating.

She squeezed him again. "The point is, things change. You may want butternut squash with all your heart, but sometimes it's kale. And it's okay if you like it, too. Because it'll never take away how much you love butternut squash."

"But there must be something we can do," he whispered.

Aggy smiled. "Oh, there is. Love them. Be there for them. Your Amelia—likely she's feeling worse about this move than you are. Comfort her. It's the noblest role of a pet. Then, be open to the possibilities of kale."

And with that, she slipped out of the room, leaving Malcolm alone in the dark. He lay in that beanbag for a long time, staring at the dark ceiling, imagining the stars above it.

He thought he might know what Aggy was asking of him: to move on. But he wasn't sure he had it in him. Eventually, though, Malcolm rolled out of the beanbag and plodded down the hall to the second grade classrooms. He knew Honey Bunny was wondering about his meeting, and Malcolm guessed he owed it to HB for going with him up to the clock tower in the first place. He'd just keep it all business. That's how Honey Bunny preferred it, anyway.

Malcolm had never been inside Honey Bunny's second grade classroom. He stopped short at the sight of Honey Bunny's cage. "Wow, they really like pink in here," Malcolm said carefully.

"The nutters think it matches my eyes," Honey Bunny said, holding the door open. He paused a second, leveling those pink eyes at Malcolm. "Don't mention it."

Malcolm nodded, but Honey Bunny poked a claw—a pointy one that had been hiding inside his silky coat—at Malcolm's chest. "No, really. *Don't* mention it."

Malcolm nodded again and started nibbling on a carrot.

Honey Bunny didn't hesitate. "So . . . what did the Striped Shadow say?"

Malcolm suddenly felt tired. The Striped Shadow. Snip. Amelia. It was all too much. "He had some actually useful information, but I think we're going to have to have all the Academy working on it around the clock." And Malcolm explained about the underlined words in the books.

"Yeah, that's a lot of books," Honey Bunny agreed. "But if we each take a couple rows, we should be able to do it. Good work. So . . . anything else?"

Malcolm shifted his eyes. "Not really. Why?"

Honey Bunny chewed for a minute. "Just wondering. Your . . . *friend* Beert seemed to think that the Striped Shadow didn't help for free."

Malcolm nodded, his mind whirring. He should tell Honey Bunny about Snip, about what Snip wanted. He knew he should ask Honey Bunny if he had lied. But it was just too much. Have you ever had that happen, Mr. Binney? Something that is all you can think about, but your thoughts are so tightly wrapped around it that you can't really put them into words? So, then, the thing you think about most—that is consuming you—is the one that nobody ever even knows about? Like moving, maybe. Even though everyone's asking you about it all day long, and you're dreading it and scared of it and hate the idea of it—*so much*—it's too hard to speak of it.

So you don't. That was Malcolm right then.

Instead, Malcolm ended up shrugging and offering an

easy lie. "He just wanted access to the dumpster. I showed him how to get in. Don't worry," he said quickly. "I made sure he knew not to leave a mess. If there's one thing the Striped Shadow is, it's smart."

Which was actually true. Which was another worry. What happens if you don't help the Shadow in return?

CHAPTER 18

A SECRET

"So what were you saying about 'bobo nickels' the other day?" It was the day before the listening session—and two days before Amelia's last day. The group was putting the final touches on their presentation and their posters, and lamenting yet again about not being able to share the time capsule or McKenna's portrait. Amelia pointed to Skylar's poster board. "Hey, you've got to use punctuation. And you spelled 'board' wrong. 'We need you bored!' means something totally different from 'We need you, Board!'" She reached over to mark the changes. "Commas matter."

Malcolm winced as Skylar rubbed out his work. In the days since her move had been announced, Amelia's mouth pinched tighter and tighter and her words stung. It was like she was *trying* to make everyone mad at her.

"It's not 'bobo'—it's 'hobo,'" Jovahn corrected gently.

Amelia frowned. "Like homeless people?"

"Kind of," Kiera answered. "But different. Mr. Binney said back in the 1930s when that nickel was made, a lot of people were out of work. They traveled all over the country, looking for jobs, riding on the trains, walking, whatever they could do. And some tried to make things to trade or sell. Like carving a nickel. That's what Mr. Binney thinks this is. He had, like, a great-uncle or someone who collected hobo nickels."

"Weird," Amelia said. "But I don't think that's going to help with our presentation—Jovahn! Can't you make that neater?"

Jovahn sighed and erased.

Amelia stared out the window. The rain had turned the snow into icy gray scabs across the playground. She kicked the table leg. Malcolm squeaked at the jolt.

She opened his cage and rubbed behind his ears. "I'm sorry, Malcolm. I just . . . we're so close! I thought we'd find the time capsule or your Loaded Stash or something. But it's like the closer we get, the foggier it gets. All we've got are some pictures and misspelled posters." She grabbed a handful of newspaper clippings. "I mean, will anyone really care how McKenna donated the land and money for the school to be built?" She jabbed her finger sarcastically.

"Oh, and don't forget how his daughter won her 'exotic South American' pet guinea pig at the Wisconsin State Fair! I'm sure that will make all the difference." She shook her head. "Somehow it felt like, if I could do this . . . Oh, never mind." She got up and walked over to the windows.

Malcolm wandered around the table, tripping over the books, markers, and scraps of paper. He knew what she was going to say: if she could save the school, somehow it wouldn't hurt as much to move from it. Malcolm knew because that's exactly how *he* felt too.

And then, he saw it. On the spine of one of the yearbooks.

A Mark!

Four triangles in a row, scratched above the date on the spine. A Marked book! It had to be. After all this time, the Midnight Academy looking through the shelves in the library—they had forgotten that some books were checked out!

Jovahn rubbed Malcolm's belly. "What's up, mousie?"

But Malcolm shook him off, instead hopping onto the yearbook. He riffled through the pages.

"Hey!" Kiera said.

Amelia turned back from the window, watching Malcolm as he wrestled with the heavy paper. "He's trying to tell us something," she said softly.

Yes, here was one! An underlined word! "In." Malcolm pointed to it with his tail. And another! "Times." The nutters stared at him. Amelia's eyebrows drew together in either a frown or a look of concentration.

Malcolm pointed to the first underlined word again. "'In,'" Amelia read aloud. "In what, Malcolm?" No! It wasn't the word "in," it was the *underlining* he wanted her to notice. He flipped back to the other page. "'Times,'" she read. She looked at him. "In times?"

Gristle! How to make her understand? He pointed to the word "times" again.

Kiera was staring with her eyes round. "Is he talking to us?! I knew it! I knew he talked to you!" she crowed. "I knew there was more going on than you just reading to him. This whole time, you've been talking. Wait until the other kids—"

Jovahn elbowed her. "You can't tell anyone!"

Amelia frowned. "Seriously, you can't. Think about if everyone knew."

Kiera paused, chomping her gum for a few seconds. "I have to keep it secret?"

Amelia and Jovahn nodded. "Even from Tianna," Jovahn said.

Kiera grumped, "That's no fun. What's the fun in knowing a secret if you can't tell it?"

Amelia rolled her eyes. "I thought the point of a secret was to keep it?"

"Of course! But, you know . . ."

Jovahn turned to Skylar. "You too, Skylar. You can't

breathe a word of this to anyone." Skylar didn't even appear to be listening, but he nodded slightly, his mouth hanging open as he stared at Malcolm.

"Skylar!" Amelia said sharply. "This is important."

Skylar jumped and focused on Amelia. He half smiled. "No. It doesn't matter. No one listens to me anyway. But, you know, I think Malcolm—"

"He's right," Kiera said. "No one can ever make sense of him. So what do you think Malcolm is saying?"

But *Malcolm* was listening. He caught Skylar's eyes. He pointed at the underlined words again: "of," "need." He flipped pages forward: "look." Malcolm traced the pencil underline. Skylar's eyes glowed. Yes! By crumb, Skylar got it.

Skylar grabbed Amelia's hand. "It's a message!" he shouted.

The three other students sighed. "We know, Skylar," Amelia said gently, trying to extract her hand. "That's what we were just saying. Malcolm can talk to us. But you can't tell anyone."

"No," said Skylar, not letting go of her. "It's not a message *from* Malcolm. There's another message. Like a code. In the book. Malcolm's trying to show us. Look." He pointed at the caption. "The word 'stars' is underlined. I read about this in a *Spy Secrets* comic once. There are other words too. If we put all the underlined words together, it'll make a message. From someone else. Not Malcolm. He's just showing it to us."

Jovahn, Kiera, and Amelia stared at one another in silence. Amelia flipped the pages back and forth. "They *are* underlined. And Malcolm doesn't underline." She pulled out a pencil.

"Malcolm, you're a genius!" crowed Jovahn, as Amelia wrote down the underlined words.

"You too, Skylar," Amelia added. Skylar flushed.

"But a message from who?" Kiera wondered.

"Whom. Let's just figure out what it is, first," Amelia said, scribbling away. "Wait, there's another one!" she said, pointing.

Malcolm had leaped off the book so that Amelia could turn the pages. With Kiera watching, he stepped onto his old notebook. He carefully pointed to the letters.

"'The Midnight Academy,'" Kiera read. "What's that?"

Amelia paused, her pencil poised above the paper. "This is a message from the Midnight Academy?" she asked Malcolm.

He nodded. "Think so," he spelled out.

"The Midnight Academy from"—Jovahn flipped to the spine of the book—"1938?"

Malcolm nodded again.

"What's the Midnight Academy?" Kiera nearly shouted.

"It's . . . kind of hard to explain," Jovahn started slowly.

"It's another secret," Amelia added. She sounded skeptical.

"It's from the story," Skylar said.

"What?" The other three turned to him.

153

"The story Mr. Binney read. Don't you remember? After *The Tale of Despereaux*, he read us that story about Malcolm here . . . It was all true, wasn't it?"

Jovahn and Amelia glanced at each other. Amelia swallowed.

Kiera darted a look from Skylar to Jovahn to Amelia. "That was a true story? All that?! The cat, the water, the . . ." Her eyes grew wide. "It *is* true, isn't it?"

Amelia slowly nodded. Kiera continued, "So if the Academy is real—whoa, you guys really mean I can't say anything about this to anyone?—Malcolm is saying this is a message from them from 1938. Well, what does it say?"

"In times of need, look beneath the oak under the stars behind McKenna."

"'Behind McKenna'? What does that mean? 'Beneath the oak'?" Jovahn asked. "I hate puzzles. Can't we just make something instead?"

"I know what it means," Amelia said softly. "Or at least part of it."

"Is it the time capsule?" Kiera asked. "But nothing was out there."

Amelia stood up straight, her eyes shining in a way they hadn't for days. "It's a message for Malcolm." She picked him up and nuzzled his ear. His tail quivered.

"It's your Loaded Stash," she whispered. "When the ground thaws out there, we're going to find your Stash."

CHAPTER 19
THE LISTENING SESSION

Malcolm raced to report the message in the yearbook to the Academy that night, but the Academy agreed that there wasn't much they could do until the ground thawed. And in the meantime, it was here: the school board listening session. The next day, the lankies were all on edge. Mrs. Whipple, the school cook, handed out ice cream bars for lunch. Before the fish sticks. It poured all day, so there was indoor recess, but not even the atomic version[1] of Heads Up, Seven Up could calm the nutters in Room 11. Nothing as crazy as Amelia forgetting her shoes happened, but

---

[1] Which Jovahn had invented. But you probably knew that.

everyone was definitely wound up. And you seemed particularly sad, Mr. Binney.

After school Ms. Brumble brought you an apple—Granny Smith—and gave you a hug. "It's going to be okay," Malcolm heard her whisper to you.

You took a bite of the apple. "They just have their hopes so tied up in this presentation tonight. And I'm not sure a bunch of kids is going to matter. Sure, the school board will listen, but the bottom line is the bottom line. There's not enough money to keep this school running the way we need it to." You sighed. "I'm not even hungry." You tossed your apple across the room to the garbage can. It missed.

"Hey! Someone has to clean up those messes, you know," Ms. Brumble said, going over pick it up and put it in the trash. "I wouldn't count out anything. Let's see what happens."

Malcolm, who had been racing on his tail-safe exercise wheel, slowed. There it was again: money. Malcolm wondered—and wished he could ask you—what would it take, really, to keep the school open? To keep Amelia here? Even if the Academy found the Loaded Stash, would it be enough? Or were they simply keeping busy like Amelia was on her presentation, and in the end whatever they found wouldn't matter because the problem was insurmountable in the first place? Malcolm felt a little like he was playing a game in which he didn't understand all the rules (not unlike Atomic Heads Up, Seven Up). And it was hard to win if you didn't even know what you were playing.

At the Midnight Academy meeting, it had been agreed that a representative needed to attend the hearing to report back. Instead of the district Midnight Academy giving them an email briefing, like they usually did after a school board meeting, McKenna's critters would report back the details of the meeting to them. Honey Bunny had been nominated for this, but when they investigated, there just wasn't a good place for a large white rabbit to hide without being seen. The same was true for Aggy and Harriet, and even Tank and Polly. Billy and Jesse were too distractible to be reliable, and everyone was too worried that Octavius or Pete might get stepped on accidentally. So that left Malcolm.

"Remember," Aggy had told him. "You are representing the Midnight Academy. We need your report to plan our next steps." Malcolm wasn't sure, but he thought she was hinting that he might be almost as distractible as Billy and Jesse. He couldn't imagine why.

So that night found Malcolm in the upper level of the auditorium (which he learned was called the balcony), overlooking the proceedings. The balcony wasn't open to the humans for the meeting, so it was the perfect hiding place. And, if someone came to check on the projector that was up there, Malcolm would just dart under a chair or in a shadow. There should be plenty of warning—enough for him to hide.

Malcolm got up there early, and soon realized that crouching on the balcony railing itself gave him the best view. He glanced up at the wall next to him. If the little rat map in his head was right (and it always was), at the top corner of the balcony's wall was Sylvia's nest. Malcolm wondered if Sylvia or her squirrelings would be able to hear the meeting.

A rumble from outside slightly shook the banister under Malcolm. Malcolm knew that sound. Thunder. So it was still raining outside. But Malcolm could already guess that—below him people were starting to trickle in to the meeting, their collars up and shaking water from their umbrellas.

At the front of the auditorium, right below and facing the stage, eight lankies sat at a long table. According to Aggy, this would be the school board. They were the ones who ultimately would decide to close McKenna or not. The risers and props from the fifth grade musical were gone; only a podium and microphone sat on the stage. Malcolm was nervous for his nutters. They'd be so alone up there!

Malcolm saw Jovahn arrive first—in pressed jeans and a button-down shirt. Then Kiera appeared behind him, in ruffles and bows, tapping him on the shoulder. She pointed at the posters that hung from the front of the stage. "We ❤ our school." "90 Years of History." "Keep McKenna Open." "We need you, Board!"

Skylar arrived next, dripping a little, with an older woman—his Gram? He wore a suit and tie. Malcolm had never seen him look so grown-up. But where was Amelia? The nutters signed in with the board to get on the schedule to speak, then took seats in the front of the room.

Finally, a tall man with a drooping white mustache and green suspenders sitting at the end of the school board table stood, climbed the stairs to the stage, and took the microphone. "Good evening," he said, stooping a little to aim his words into the microphone. "Welcome. We're here tonight to get some feedback from you—the Clearwater community—about what to do with this school." He gestured widely. "It's been proposed that it may be time to move on. I'll admit, I attended this school and it breaks my heart to speak of possibly closing it. But in these hard financial times . . . well, it's important for us—your school board—to be good stewards of your money."

Not all of that made sense to Malcolm, partly because he was distracted by the arrival of Amelia. She took his breath away. Her long black hair hung shiny and loose down her back. She shrugged out of her raincoat and slid into a seat next to Jovahn. Malcolm wasn't sure, but he thought he saw her parents take a seat behind Skylar's Gram.

The tall lanky up front continued. "Perhaps the weather has delayed some of us . . ." He frowned a little. He was right, Malcolm realized. Besides the school board, the seats were only full until about halfway up. Malcolm felt a little pang of panic. Didn't more people care about this? "But I'd like us to get started. We'll begin with the financial report from our head of Building and Grounds, Robert Larson."

Mr. Larson spoke at length about what Malcolm mostly knew already from the last district Midnight Academy report. The series of broken windows, the broken pipe and subsequent flooded basement, something new about the ventilation system and WiFi, and now the electrical issues. As Mr. Larson brought this up, there was a clap of thunder and the lights flickered. The audience twittered.

The next person up spoke about the enrollment at McKenna and how, every year, there were fewer students in McKenna's neighborhood. Also, how there was plenty of room at Fairfax and Parkview, if they split the school and bused the students there. There were a lot of complicated graphs and charts and maps. Malcolm closed his eyes just for a second. When would they get to something interesting? Like Amelia?

Ping.

Malcolm's ears pricked up. What was that?

Ping. Ping.

He sniffed. But all he could smell was wetness. The rain outside was still pouring down. Thunder shook the building and the lights flickered again just as Mrs. Rivera, McKenna's principal, took the stage.

Ping. Ping. Pingpingpingping. Taptaptap. The noise was getting faster. And louder. And it was coming from the roof—the side of the auditorium where Sylvia's nest was. Malcolm crept over to her corner and up the decorative carvings on the wall (like only a rat could). The plaster under his feet was cool and damp. Here he could see her hole—a crack in the plaster, really. It was hard to tell, but there seemed to be a shadowy patch stretching from the corner across the ceiling. He watched as a single drop of water ran down the slope of the ceiling to the light fixture in the center of the auditorium. There it formed a drop and fell on the crowd below.

Oh, gristle.

But that wasn't the worst of it. The worst was when Malcolm crawled back down the wall to listen as Amelia's group took the stage.

Because when he turned around, there, on the far edge of the balcony, was Snip.

CHAPTER 20

RATS!

Malcolm wobbled on the balcony railing. He glanced below; Amelia was leading the All-Stars up the stage's steps. He turned back to Snip. "You! How'd you get in here?"

"Shhh!" the cat said. "Do you want all those tall ones to hear you?" She ruffled her fur and turned her back to him. "You are not the only one with access to the building, you know."

"Someone let you in? Who? Why?" Malcolm walked closer. He tested himself. His tail was not quaking. He didn't feel that blinding fear inside anymore that made him want to run like a nutter with a bee in his shirt. Snip was just . . . a cat. Granted, Malcolm was still a rat and remained interested in not being eaten, but all that Kiera-like drama Snip used to bring out in him was . . . gone. Malcolm wondered if it was because he had now found out that there were worse things that could happen to him than her.

She arched her back, and Malcolm saw that she really did look a lot more healthy than the scary-skinny cat she had been on the fourth floor. Her coat was shiny and filled in. For a brief moment, Malcolm wondered where she lived, how she lived outside. She was definitely eating more than spiders and dust.

She scoffed. "What's with all the questions? Let's just say there are other favors floating about. And clearly, you have never been Outside for any extended period. There's this thing called 'rain.' It's where water pours from the sky." She shuddered. "I don't like water."

"But—but, where?" As far as Malcolm knew, the only ways into the building were through a main entrance (unlikely), the clock tower, or—

Snip nodded toward the back corner.

Now a niggle of fear wormed its way into Malcolm's stomach. "You came in through Sylvia's nest? Is she okay?"

"Sylvia?" Snip repeated. "Is that the name of that nut-brained squirrel? Yeah, she got what she wanted."

What did that mean? But before Malcolm could ask, someone *else* wiggled through the hole in the wall (which had—as you might expect after a cat had used it—grown quite a bit). More plaster fell to the floor in chunks. What the crumb? Had the whole Outside world been given an invitation to this listening session too?

It was the raccoon who had led Malcolm to the Striped Shadow in the deserted tire factory! The raccoon—what had been his name? Acer?—bumbled in on his three paws, his fur glistening a little from the rain. He stopped short when he saw Malcolm. Then Snip. His eyes zigged and zagged between them. Then he licked his lips. "Hello," he said slowly.

"What are *you* doing here?" Malcolm wondered, but then he didn't even wait for an answer. "Never mind! You need to get out of here! There's a meeting below! A very important meeting! With lankies and everything."

Snip snorted. She leaped up on the balcony railing with Malcolm. "Lankies." She blew out through her nose, making her whiskers jiggle. "Nutters. You and your humans. I'm not scared of them." She strolled along the balcony railing, in plain view of the audience, should anyone care to turn around and look up.

"Get down!" Malcolm whispered, running toward her. "They'll see you!"

"Will they?" Snip stretched and added a little meow.

Malcolm lunged at her. "Be quiet!" He checked below. A very small nutter, sitting on his mother's lap, turned his head and glanced up.

Snip dodged and leaped over Malcolm on the railing,

mewing again. The nutter boy below waved. "Kitty," he called.

Malcolm spun around to face Snip and teetered dangerously. Either someone had polished the railing, or dust was very slippery. Snip could not ruin this meeting for Amelia! Malcolm said the only thing he could think of. "If you don't care about them so much, why do you want to come back inside? You hated it in here. You hated the lankies. You hated the nutters. You even hated us, the Midnight Academy."

Snip paused. She hissed. "You're wrong. I *especially* hated the Midnight Academy."

"So why come back?" Malcolm couldn't understand it. "There's nothing for you here."

Snip stared at him for what seemed like at least two hours. Then she raised her lips to show her sharp teeth and hissed again. "I want back in because it's all I've got. It's all I know."

"So you want it even though it makes you miserable? And—" Malcolm wheeled around on Acer. "Is that why *you're* here? Are you here to help the Striped Shadow with Snip?"

"Help the Striped Shadow?" Snip laughed. "Oh, Malcolm. To live in your small, small world. He's not *helping* the Striped Shadow; he—"

"Whoa—ho!" Acer, who had been watching this whole exchange, made a surprisingly graceful three-pawed leap onto the railing too. "I think it's time to go, Blackberry. I didn't know there was a meeting here tonight."

"Didn't you? I thought you knew everything."

Malcolm glanced below. By now, the small nutter had the row of people behind and in front of him looking up and pointing. When Acer made an appearance on the railing, his shape blocked the stream of light from the projector. Now a giant shadow of a raccoon blocked the projection of Jovahn's slide at the front of the auditorium. The whole room turned and looked up at the balcony.

But that didn't stop Snip. "Don't we need to tell the truth here? Isn't that part of your promise under the stars? I thought you—"

Whatever it was she thought, Acer didn't let her finish. He charged at her. She ran to the end of the balcony, leaping over Malcolm again, and onto the velvet drapes that hung on the wall next to it. Her claws dragged through them, but her weight was too much. The drapes ripped, and she made a slow descent to the main floor, amid gasps and screams from the audience. No one was watching the stage anymore.

Acer chased after her, but he wasn't expecting Malcolm to be in the way. He couldn't stop in time, and he plowed right into Malcolm as he followed Snip to the drapes. "Sorry!" he shouted over his shoulder.

But sorry wasn't enough, because Malcolm was falling. The blow knocked him clean off the balcony railing to the audience below.

Malcolm had a soft landing, at least—in the lap of an elderly man. He jumped up as Malcolm landed on him. When the man saw what Malcolm was, he stood and shrieked, "Rats! Rats!" He brushed Malcolm off and flung him to the floor.

Oh, sure! Of all the times for a lanky to finally recognize what Malcolm really was! Malcolm would have liked to stay and explain: It wasn't "rats," anyway; it was "rat." Just one, who actually lived here at McKenna, but not in the way the lanky was thinking.

Screeching "mouse" would have been bad enough, but it wouldn't have had the same reaction that "rats" did. The audience erupted. Snip and Acer had made it to the floor and were racing up an aisle. Malcolm chased after them. Chairs flapped and folded as people moved to get out of the way of the critters.

Snip took a turn up the main aisle, Acer followed, and Malcolm brought up the rear. He didn't understand all that had happened in the balcony, but he figured that Snip, of any critter, would know the best way to get out of this room. Which seemed really key right about now. Getting out without getting stepped on, preferably. Malcolm dodged as he ran. The audience was on their feet now, people hastily pulling coats and gloves on and storming up the aisles.

Up front, Kiera paused. She smoothed her hair back. Amelia nudged her. It was possible that the nutters couldn't see the pandemonium[1] that was erupting in the audience. Jovahn clicked to the next slide. Kiera continued, but without the typical confidence in her voice. "We found out that there is a time capsule that was buried in 1938. When the ground thaws . . ."

And that's when the little *pingpingping* drip became a trickle. Then a pour, and then, with a sound not unlike nutters messing around in the restroom, a splash. And a chunk of plaster fell from the ceiling, landing in the aisle in front of Malcolm. He reared up to stop suddenly. Snip and Acer, oblivious to what was happening behind them,

---

[1] Vocabulary from 3/1. Chaos. I know we are not supposed to define a vocabulary word with another, but chaos and pandemonium are really the only way to describe what happened that night. Unless you want me to use a simile. The crowd was like popcorn popping. Screaming popcorn.

headed for the outside door, which someone had mercifully propped open.

Then—*splash!* And *crash!*

The *splash-crash* was like a pause button in the room. Everyone turned and saw what amounted to a small waterfall pouring from the light fixture to the aisle below. Next to the light, bare wooden patches showed through where the plaster had fallen to the floor.

The tall lanky on the school board, who had been trying to wrestle his way to the front of the room against the tide of people who had decided it was time to leave, finally made it there. He gestured frantically at someone in the back, and the audience lights went on. Now the nutters on the stage could see what was happening. Malcolm watched as Amelia's eyes followed the water from the ceiling to the floor and then to him. They grew wide, and Malcolm saw her mouth form his name.

"There's the rat!" someone yelled, and Malcolm jumped into action again. Someone tried to throw a scarf over him, and he dodged, dashing under a chair in an empty aisle, panting.

He didn't know what to think. Everything ruined. Snip. Acer. The rain. The nutters' presentation. And water. Again.

The tall lanky took the microphone from Kiera and said, "Um, I think under tonight's circumstances, we'll have to—" Just then, another chunk of plaster broke off and fell, and the people in the audience started walking out faster.

". . . adjourn for tonight. Perhaps we can reschedule this meeting—"

And that was when another enormous clap of thunder shook the room, and the lights flickered out for good.

CHAPTER 21
SCHOOL'S CLOSED

You know that feeling when you first wake up and before you even see a clock, you know you've overslept? Something about the light is weird, or maybe it's too quiet, or possibly you're starving more than you usually are.

That's how Malcolm woke up. With a start that jolted him upright, knocking his head on his water bottle. With wet ears.

The light was wrong in Room 11. It was still raining outside, but it wasn't just that. The lights were off, and the clock read 7:39, but Malcolm knew it was much later. What was going on? Where were the nutters? The lankies? Had Malcolm slept through Amelia's last day? His insides felt as jangly as a pocketful of hobo coins.

Ms. Brumble walked into the room. She was on the phone and headed toward Malcolm's cage. She tapped, and Malcolm raised up on his hind legs to say hi.

"Yes, he's here. I don't think that could have been him last night at the meeting." She made a face. "I hate to say it, but maybe we do have other rats in McKenna. Some people are even saying they saw a cat. We definitely have a raccoon—and squirrels, apparently. They just cleared out a nest way up under the eaves inside the wall." She opened Malcolm's cage. "Yes, I'll refill his food and water to last through the weekend." She sprinkled some pellets down, her phone wedged between her neck and ear. A pause while she listened.

"Yes, he's warm enough! There are emergency generators, you know. That's why I'm here early today. But they're hoping to open back on Monday. The lightning hit the tree on the side of the school. You know that huge oak? You should see it. Just shattered. Hold on—" She pressed a button on her phone, and your voice echoed in the room.

"The Council Oak? Oh no! It was so crazy getting out of there last night, I didn't even see it. How's the auditorium look today?" you asked through the phone.

"Well, it's a mess," Ms. Brumble called from the sink across the room where she was refilling Malcolm's water bottle. "I don't see it being used for a while. They've got to repair the roof—there are bricks loose in the corner where the auditorium joins the rest of the school. That's where the water came in. That raccoon, too, apparently. Quite a lot of damage. That's all going to take longer than Monday, I'm afraid."

Malcolm groomed his back paws, trying to pretend he wasn't listening carefully. The Council Oak got hit by lightning? But what about the message "In times of need, look beneath the oak under the stars behind McKenna"? Was the Loaded Stash destroyed before they could even find it? And what about Sylvia and her squirrelings if her nest had been pulled down? And where had Acer and Snip ended up? It was too much. For a moment, Malcolm wished he was back asleep again. Then he stopped, mid-groom. What had Ms. Brumble said? Open Monday? Did that mean . . . ?

That was why it was so quiet today. No school. Somehow the electricity going out had them cancel school. And it was Amelia's last day. Malcolm's day to say goodbye to her.

A panicky feeling bloomed in Malcolm's stomach. This wasn't it, was it? Amelia would come back on Monday to say goodbye, right?

Malcolm heard you sigh through the phone. "Two days closed this year because of the condition of the building. Of all the times for all this to happen. They're never going to vote to keep McKenna open now."

Ms. Brumble hung Malcolm's water bottle and closed his cage. Her lips pressed together. "I know," she said softly.

There was silence between you for a moment that

scared Malcolm more than even seeing Snip alive again. Ms. Brumble picked up the phone. She pressed another button, brought the phone to her ear, and headed back out the door. "I guess we have to hope for some good news."

Malcolm lay on his back in his cage for the rest of the day and evening, staring up at the ceiling tiles. It's a very unnatural position for rats to be in—it exposes their soft bellies to any sort of predators.

But Malcolm didn't care. What was the point? Amelia was gone. The school was doomed. The stupid legend of Ernie Bowman had gone nowhere. A Loaded Stash for times of need! One junky Niche had been all they'd found —full of stuff more useless than the scraps and comics at the bottom of Skylar's desk. And those poor nutters. All that time on their presentation, and it was ruined by a rat and a soggy ceiling.

The Midnight Academy bell rang, and Malcolm remembered he was supposed to give a report to the district Academy.

He didn't budge. Finally, Honey Bunny came by.

"Hey, rat," Honey Bunny said, hopping up onto Malcolm's table. "You missed the meeting."

Malcolm rolled over so his back was to the rabbit. He buried his face in his paper scraps.

Honey Bunny waited, then said, "We heard how the

meeting ended last night. The district would still like your official report about it eventually. Octavius said he'd help you type it up in an email, if you want."

There was a long pause. Finally, Malcolm nodded.

Honey Bunny cleared his throat. "Hey," he said, his voice gruffer than usual. "That's rough, not being able to say goodbye." He swallowed. "I know."

Malcolm turned toward Honey Bunny then. Honey Bunny's ears drooped even more than usual. He *did* know, Malcolm remembered.

"Yeah," Malcolm said in a whisper. He hardly trusted his voice, but he asked, "What's going to happen now?"

Honey Bunny lay down on the table so he was eye to eye with Malcolm. "We go on. Like Aggy said, there is no shortage of nutters who need us. No one will ever replace Amelia, but surely you can think of others — maybe even in your classroom now — who need a friend."

Skylar's face flashed before Malcolm's eyes. And, for some reason, Snip's. But Malcolm pushed them away. "I don't think I could do it again," Malcolm said finally.

Honey Bunny nodded. "Maybe not now, but — well, I've seen you in action, Malcolm. You have too good a heart to not help people. You know how Jesse teases you about your 'hero brain'? Well, there's 'hero heart,' too. I'm afraid you've got both." Honey Bunny sat up. "And besides, we have work to do. The Loaded Stash is still out there."

Malcolm rolled over. "What's the point? I heard the

175

lankies talking today. They'll never vote to keep the school open after last night's disaster."

"Oh, Malcolm. You haven't been in the Academy all that long. You have no idea how many times the lankies don't know exactly what they need to know until the Academy helps them to see it. So let's find that Stash. Harriet went out through the basement and tried an experimental dig outside tonight. Sure, the tree is down, but that doesn't mean there's not a Loaded Stash out there like the message said. It'll turn up. You'll see. And you never know, it might be what McKenna needs. There's a reason Ernie Bowman hid it. Come on, now. Time to stop wallowing. We need you. All of us do."

And with that, Honey Bunny hopped off the table and left, leaving Malcolm to think it over. Nutters and critters worse off than he was? Yes, maybe. But that didn't make Malcolm hurt less. Still, after all he had heard today —Sylvia's nest being cleaned out, the Council Oak being hit by lightning, even Harriet going Outside (!)—well, it was time for Malcolm to see for himself what exactly was going on.

CHAPTER 22

PAID IN FULL

Malcolm couldn't get out of the school through Sylvia's nest anymore. Ms. Brumble hadn't been kidding when she said the lankies were working on repairing the auditorium. In the end, he went up to the clock tower, bonged the clock, and got another ride from Beert.

Malcolm had wanted to see what the tree looked like, and as Beert banked and glided past it, a shiver ran through him.

The lankies had cut down the giant. It lay sprawled across the muddy gray-brown grass, cut in chunks, like how Tianna cut up her hot dog before eating it with a fork.

A charred black streak ran the length of it, and it smelled faintly of matches.[1]

Malcolm hopped off Beert and waved. "It's okay. I just want to look around a bit."

"All right," the owl said. "I'm going to swoop the jogging path down by the river. Pick you up in a few minutes?"

Malcolm nodded.

It was much harder going than the last time he had been out here. Then, there had been snow that Malcolm could walk over. Now, the snow was gone and what was left was gummy mud. Soon Malcolm was coated up to his eyeballs. He crawled over the blackened trunk of the tree. It had been so wide that Malcolm was now several feet in the air. He walked down the length of it and couldn't help thinking that this was another part of McKenna that was gone forever.

Malcolm came to a crook in the branches and stopped. The "dwell here" Mark was half gone, shredded when the branches had fallen. Looking at it, Malcolm realized that Amelia and, potentially, the Midnight Academy were not the only ones who were losing their homes. What animals had lived in the huge branches of the Council Oak? Of course, there were other trees, but those Outside critters

---

[1] Malcolm knew of matches from science experiments. He also knew what burning erasers smelled like. And melted plastic. Those were not supposed to be part of the science experiments.

probably felt the same way about their Council Oak home as Malcolm did about Room 11.

Maybe Honey Bunny was right. Malcolm needed to stop feeling sorry for himself.

As he continued on into what had been the upper branches, an argument from the ground below filled his ears.

"No refunds. No redos." Malcolm recognized the Striped Shadow's voice. As usual, he was lurking in the shadows of the branches. He sure took his name seriously!

"But you promised! Aren't you as good as your word?" Malcolm heard Sylvia say. *Sylvia?* Well, he supposed that made sense. She was the one who had told him about the Striped Shadow, after all, and now that her nest was gone, she was probably desperate for a new one for her squirrelings. Malcolm turned to slip away. He didn't need to hear her negotiations.

"I *am* as good as my word." The raccoon's whispery voice was dangerous. "I provided you with a nest like you asked for—Inside, no less."

"But it's gone now! And I still helped you! I let that cat in the building. Can't you see how you still owe me?"

Malcolm's heart thumped in his chest. What had she said? *Sylvia* had let Snip in? Suddenly, Malcolm could see: when he had refused, the Striped Shadow must have gone to Sylvia, who apparently still owed him. If there was anything the Shadow was about, it was keeping up his business model. He couldn't have Snip going around saying he didn't keep his promises. And Sylvia probably didn't even know what she had done. Her only concern had ever been for her squirrelings.

The Shadow sighed. Malcolm heard the rattle of dry oak leaves as they moved away. "Fine," the Shadow said. "But it's almost spring now. Why do you even need me? Take your pick of any tree."

Malcolm jumped down off the branches to follow them, wanting to hear where exactly Snip was *now*. The ground was soft here too. Both the Striped Shadow and Sylvia had left their footprints in the mud.

Malcolm paused. Their footprints. The smaller, shallower ones must be Sylvia's. But the Striped Shadow's looked almost like little nutter hands with their five fingers.

But that wasn't what made Malcolm stop. It was the number of prints. The Striped Shadow—and that had clearly been the Striped Shadow's voice—had only three paws.

Just like . . . Acer.

Malcolm remembered the night before. Snip's confusion, Acer not letting her talk.

Acer wasn't *working* for the Striped Shadow.

Acer *was* the Striped Shadow!

"Figured it out, huh?" said Acer/the Striped Shadow from behind the oak's branches—he was using Acer's voice now, not the dramatic, deep whisper that the Striped Shadow used.

Malcolm turned. The Striped Shadow—Acer—was looking directly at him. Sylvia was gone.

"But—but—why?" Malcolm sputtered. "You help people. Why hide it?"

"It's the reputation," Acer said, climbing out of the shadows finally to sit by Malcolm. "Who's going to come to a young raccoon for help? A three-legged raccoon, at that? I'm not a fixer without the name. I'm only Acer, the raccoon who was dumb enough to get his paw caught and is lucky to be alive. But the Striped Shadow? Well, he can do anything. The real Striped Shadow retired ages ago. I took over after about . . ." He counted on his paw. "The seventh. The last Striped Shadow trained me. And I'll train the next, and the Striped Shadow will live on as the legendary Outside fixer."

Malcolm's mouth hung open. "So no other critters know?"

Acer shook his head. "Only you."

Malcolm swallowed. "And maybe . . . Snip."

Acer made a face. "Yeah, I really messed that up. When I first met with her, I never thought I'd be doing business again with an Inside critter, so I let her see me. The business model is to stick to the shadows so if you run into customers, they don't recognize you. But then you came along."

Malcolm nodded toward Acer's missing paw. "How did you lose it?"

"Last year. I snuck into the factory and boxes fell on me.

181

I was in rough shape. But it was the Striped Shadow who found me. Saved me. And eventually trained me. And now, that's me."

"Where is the old Striped Shadow?"

Acer got a faraway look in his eyes. He gestured behind him. "He's gone downriver now," he said quietly.

Malcolm wasn't sure what that meant exactly. But then, he figured, maybe it didn't matter. Because what it meant to Acer was that he was gone.

Like Amelia.

Acer broke the silence. He cleared his throat. "What I was trying to say is if you keep my secret, we'll call it even. You've paid your favor."

"Really? That's it?" Malcolm said. He couldn't believe how he had gone from having to help Snip to just keeping his mouth shut. "It's not much of a favor. I don't know who I'd tell anyway."

Acer nodded, studying the rat for a minute, until Malcolm squirmed. Finally, Acer said, "Have you Inside critters found that Loaded Stash yet?"

Malcolm leaped up. "No. Why? Do you know something else? Because we *are* really, truly desperate." He waved at the exploded tree. "This caused us problems Inside, too."

"I don't, I'm sorry—and the old Striped Shadow would be cuffing me on the head right now for admitting that, but it's the truth. If you want my advice—which people ask for a lot less frequently—it sounds like you need to talk to someone who has been through the history of the school."

Malcolm sat back down slowly. "We have. Aggy and Harriet don't know," Malcolm said sadly. "And they've been here the longest."

"Huh," Acer said, getting up to leave. He switched to his whispery Shadow voice. "Too bad there isn't someone else. Someone who's also been at McKenna a long time. Listening . . . hurting." Malcolm could barely hear that last word as the Striped Shadow leaped onto the trunk of a maple nearby.

Malcolm leaned back. "I know what you're doing!" he nearly shouted up at the tree. "I know who you mean! But I'm not going to talk to Snip. I can't. Do you have Jell-O for brains? Apart from everything she's done in the past, she just single-handedly destroyed the meeting last night. Thanks to her, I didn't get to say goodbye to my nutter. You think you miss the last Striped Shadow? That's nothing to how I miss Amelia. And now there's more reason than ever to vote to close the school. Snip's ruined everything. Everything she's ever been a part of has gone wrong."

His words echoed in the quiet night. Acer didn't answer. Malcolm hunched his shoulders. He shouldn't have said that about the old Striped Shadow. While Malcolm didn't think it was possible to feel worse than he did, Acer certainly could feel as bad, and Malcolm wouldn't wish that on anyone. Then, just as Malcolm was about to leave, he heard words from above.

"I know," the Striped Shadow said. "And *she* knows it too."

Then he disappeared into the branches of the maple.

CHAPTER 23

UNDER the STARS AGAIN

After Beert dropped him back off, Malcolm hunkered in his cage, overwhelmed with Snip, the building closing, and Amelia. But as the weekend passed, his tail started twitching. What would Monday bring? Finally, late Sunday night, he popped his cage and wandered the halls.

He found himself at the auditorium. He could already smell the wet wood and plaster. He squeezed under the door and climbed up on the balcony railing to look below. A tall ladderlike structure stretched to the ceiling, and huge fans roared as they blasted air at the wet seats.

With a pang, Malcolm glanced at the stage where he had last seen Amelia. Where she had mouthed his name. Was that the last time they would see each other? She didn't even get all the goodbye notes from Room 11—not even Malcolm's, which he had pasted together from nibbling out words from a magazine (with Jovahn's assistance—glue is very tricky for rats).

And all that work Amelia, Jovahn, Kiera, and Skylar had put into their presentation! Looking for the time capsule. McKenna's history. "The stars of our class," you had called them, Mr. Binney. "Rescuing our school." And for what? Not a single person in the audience had heard what they had had to say. They were too distracted by a rat falling out of the ceiling.

"The stars of our class." Your words echoed in Malcolm's head as he stared at the stage. The *stars* . . . Malcolm sat up with a jolt. Like she was next to him, he heard Amelia scolding Skylar about "bored" and "board." Words did have different meanings, sometimes. *Stars.* Jovahn was the school basketball *star.* And apparently, there were movie *stars*—Tianna talked about them all the time. What if the yearbook message meant a different kind of star?

Suddenly, Malcolm's feet began to sweat as he remembered the rest of Amelia's scolding. What if "beneath the oak under the stars behind McKenna" didn't mean one Loaded Stash, outside under the Council Oak? What if there were . . . Malcolm tried to remember what those little marks in writing were that Amelia got so excited about. Commas. "Commas matter," Amelia had said. It had changed the meaning of Skylar's sign. What if commas could change *this* meaning?

Malcolm tried it. *"Beneath the oak, under the stars, behind McKenna."*

There could be three places, not one.

And if "under the stars" meant *Inside* rather than *Outside* . . . He glanced at the stage. Could it mean stars of the stage?

He had to find out. So he took the quickest way down. He leaped onto the velvet wall hanging (you have to admit, how Snip and Acer got down the night before looked like too much fun not to try it) and zipped up the aisle.

The stage looked even bigger right beneath it. Huge. Malcolm climbed up the steps onto it and looked out at the audience seats. It was so vast that he wasn't sure how Amelia had done it, had gotten up in front of everyone. If anyone did, *she* had hero brain — doing something that scary for a school she wasn't even going to anymore.

Malcolm bounced on his toes. So . . . this was where the "stars" stood. Now, how to get "under" them?

He raced back and forth on the smooth wooden surface of the stage, sniffing along, scanning for a Mark. Nothing. He climbed back down the steps and stood facing the stage again.

And that's when he spied it. At the base of the stage, on the left-hand side: 1938. The year on the yearbook and the second hobo nickel. Malcolm reached out a paw and scratched the mortar with a claw. Just like the bricks in the wall above, it crumbled like sand. As he scratched, he noticed something on the wall, etched into the brick below the date. A Mark. "This is the place"—like the Sign outside the Striped Shadow's headquarters.

Malcolm scratched harder. And soon, the whole stone was loose. But it wasn't even a whole stone, it was a shallow stone facing, and as Malcolm chipped away at the mortar, the 1938 fell right off the wall.

Another hollow. A Niche. Or a Loaded Stash?

Malcolm dove in.

It was a shallow space with only one thing filling it: a smooth metal box. As Malcolm looked for the latch, the box seemed familiar, like he had seen it before. But where?

He found the latch, and—by bracing himself against the wall of the space and shoving hard—he popped it open.

He read the note inside: "Welcome, future students! This time capsule was buried to honor the construction of our new auditorium and gymnasium in the fall of 1938." Malcolm almost laughed. He had found the time capsule! And then he almost cried. Because the very first person —the only person, really—he wanted to tell about it, he couldn't. He had no way of letting Amelia know that they had been successful. That it had been her commas, in fact, that had made the discovery possible.

To distract himself, he nosed through the box. Maybe there was still a bag of gold or a magic wand in there somewhere. What he found instead—amid a yellowed newspaper, a flag with the letter *C* emblazoned on it, a list of all the students, some photos, and a 1937 Clearwater yearbook—was an envelope.

"A message from Mr. Walton McKenna. October 17, 1938" was written in long, slanting letters that reminded Malcolm of Tianna's notes when she wrote them "fancy."

A message from the man himself? Would it tell what had happened to his missing money?

Well, would you be able to wait, Mr. Binney? Malcolm couldn't. He nibbled the envelope open. (He figured no one could prove he'd done it, anyway. Who's to say another rat, over the many years, hadn't gnawed on the letter?) Then he dragged the letter out to the floor in front of the stage to read it.

Dear Clearwater of the Future,

They asked me to write something to add to this time capsule. But I'm not sure what to say. All I've ever done is inherit money, nothing truly important.

So I will tell you a secret instead. A story.

Over my lifetime, I've enjoyed giving my money away. Building important things, like the library, the courthouse, and this addition to the school. But nothing has given me as much satisfaction as what I did with my money last week.

Malcolm's whiskers twanged. Here it was! Finally.

It began with a traveler, a hobo. Being so close to the train tracks, we were used to having them stop in, asking for food, looking for odd jobs. This one was no different. Except that he showed up with a blue jay on his shoulder and said he was an artist—he even offered a carved nickel in exchange for bread and said that he could whittle or paint—anything we liked.

Well, my daughter was enchanted with the nickel— it was a miniature portrait of the traveler's dog. So my wife put him to work painting the fence. It probably wasn't what he had in mind, but he did it without complaining.

He stayed with us for a week. On the night that he was set to go, I heard a noise in the yard. At first I thought it was the dogs. But then I saw there was someone back there near the fence line. Well, I don't know how things are for you in the future, but right now, if you put your money in a bank, there is a chance you'll never see it again. That's one of the reasons I stayed comfortable through the troubles. My money was in many places. And none of them was a bank.

But one of my places was under a fence post in the backyard. I hurried out. Imagine my surprise when I caught the traveler red-handed: the fence post dug up and my Mason jar full of money in his hand. He was so startled, he dropped it, smashing the glass on the ground.

At first, anger flared up in me. I had trusted him. We had chatted all week as I went to and from work. I had learned about his younger brother in Milwaukee, how he had saved his bird's life, how he and his dog first met. How dare he!

His dog ran to greet me, then nudging my hand with his nose. I opened my mouth—to yell, to call the police, to holler for the missus, but I couldn't do it. Because I saw the man's feet. And I saw how, even though he had spent a week sleeping in my shed, painting my fence, carving my daughter's guinea pig on a nickel, his boots had holes in them. And his pants—they were held up with twine! How could I have missed this?

Here I was, building these big important things. Things

with my name on them, with money I didn't even earn. And I didn't see the obvious.

So I handed him the money. All of it. I tucked it in his shirt pocket. He was so surprised that he ran, his big goofy dog loping after him.

I know how he spent part of the money—I saw him the next day enjoying a hearty meal, with new boots on his feet and bright red suspenders over his shoulders. And I knew I had done the right thing, because I watched him as he took that money and bought a comic book for a boy who had just been kicked out of the newsstand for reading without paying.

So I leave you with this thought, future Clearwater students: Sometimes you have to give people not what they're asking for, but what they need. And it's up to you to notice it. And do something about it.

Sincerely,

Mr. Walton McKenna

Malcolm sat for a long time after reading that note, thinking. This "traveler" had to be—could only be— Ernie Bowman. All the parts of the story were there—the dog on the silver coin, the rescued bird, the suspenders, the money. Malcolm smiled. Even the granting of wishes! He'd bet anything that part came from buying a boy a comic book.

So Malcolm had found the time capsule. And he had

found Ernie Bowman. Malcolm thought back to the story they had read of Clearwater High School's mascot, of the blue jay who lived in the library. Could it be the same bird? That bird had been rescued by a handyman. Had Ernie Bowman stayed in Clearwater? Could the yearbook have gotten his name wrong? Malcolm pondered it. It was possible. Maybe they didn't have someone like Amelia to check the details.

What was still out there, though, was the Loaded Stash. Because if the time capsule was "under the stars," then surely, either "beneath the oak" and "behind McKenna" had to be this money of McKenna's. The Loaded Stash.

Malcolm grinned. So they weren't too late. If money was what ran the humans' world, maybe it was what would save their school after all.

But first, he'd let the nutters "find" the time capsule. He paused in packing up the letter. The Midnight Academy needed to see this. It was their legend, after all. And if he left the letter with the rest of the time capsule, they wouldn't get to read it. So Malcolm picked up the pages and tucked them under a chair in the audience (row A, seat 11). The rest of the time capsule, though . . . well, he'd have to leave it all right there—there wasn't any way he could put the stone back. But, hopefully, the lankies and nutters would figure out what it was. They may wonder how it got out of the wall, but Malcolm guessed they'd skip over that part with the excitement of finally finding it.

After Malcolm had finished tucking it all away the best he could, he looked up. And flinched. Snip!—watching him from the balcony, her yellow eyes gleaming.

She spoke first, calling out across the big space. "I'm staying in here. You can't stop me. But I will say this: I *did* hate the nutters, the lankies, and the Midnight Academy. But this time, well . . . I'll stay out of your way, if you stay out of mine."

Then she slipped down off the railing and out of sight. Malcolm hadn't even had time to answer, to ask her again why she would want to come back to where she had been so unhappy. Where no one wanted her.

And then it was a line from McKenna's letter echoed in his head.

Sometimes you have to give people not what they're asking for, but what they need.

Malcolm snorted. How would *that* fit in with the Striped Shadow's business model? But at the same time, it made him pause. Why had he thought of that just then?

And then he Knew. He and Snip actually *wanted* the same thing—for things not to change. Only . . . in Snip's case, maybe staying wasn't what she *needed.*

And it's up to you to notice it. And do something about it.

Malcolm would have to think about that part.

CHAPTER 24
THE CODE

Monday morning came. Without Amelia at Malcolm's table, there was a squabble about who got to sit next to him now. In the end, you drew names, Mr. Binney, and Skylar won. Malcolm quickly noticed that perhaps the reason Skylar so very rarely knew what was going on was because he was constantly reading comics. He hid them in his binder. And if he wasn't reading them, he was drawing them.

The class was as glum as Malcolm felt. You had explained, Mr. Binney, that you would send the class's cards over to Amelia at her new school, so she would get them. Michael raised his hand and asked about the cupcakes you and Ms. Brumble were going to bring as a goodbye treat.

"Well," you said, "Ms. Brumble did bake them. I suppose they're still in the teachers' lounge. I guess Amelia wouldn't mind if we ate them."

But if anyone felt as bad as Malcolm, it was Jovahn. He didn't say a word all morning. Not even when Tianna announced loudly she really had to go. She meant to her locker, but still. Normally, Jovahn could not resist a joke like that. And he didn't even touch his cupcake, either. It sat on his desk for most of the afternoon, until Skylar bumped into it and it landed—frosting-side down—on Skylar's shoe.

Instead, Jovahn spent most of the day staring out the window, twisting something on his wrist. Malcolm finally caught a glimpse of it. It was a green hair elastic. Malcolm's heart panged. He knew just how Jovahn felt.

The one bright spot was near the end of the day when Ms. Brumble came in to tell you and the class that they had found the time capsule—in the auditorium, of all places! This even perked up Jovahn for a second. "But the yearbook said it was under the Council Oak," he protested.

"I know!" Ms. Brumble said. Then softer, "Trust me, I know. I guess that was the plan, but they had so much rain that week, they moved the ceremony inside. There was newspaper in the capsule that had an article about rescheduling it. I guess the change never made it into the yearbook." She squeezed Jovahn's shoulder. "Probably if you All-Stars had had another week, you guys would have figured it out."

During quiet work time, you sat down at your computer, Mr. Binney. You smiled at something. And the next thing Malcolm knew, you put a printed-out piece of paper on Malcolm's table. Skylar looked at it, then at you, Mr. Binney. The recess bell rang and the class headed out the door.

"Jovahn, Kiera, my All-Stars," you called out. "Hold on a minute." Jovahn plodded over. Kiera waved to Tianna, then joined him.

"I wanted to let you know that I heard from Amelia's new teacher today. She's doing okay. She misses you, but she's fitting in. Her teacher was wondering something, though. She said that Amelia insisted on her sending me this link. In an email. Today. Quite honestly, her new teacher also had some questions about Amelia's bossiness. I told her just to work with it." You grinned, and that even made Jovahn crack a smile, remembering all the things Amelia had been in charge of in Room 11. "Anyway, I clicked through to the webpage, and it didn't make any sense to me. So I printed it out." You pointed to the piece of paper in front of Skylar. "I'm thinking it's really for you."

"It's a code," Skylar said.

The group leaned in to peer at the paper. Malcolm couldn't see! He climbed to the top of his exercise wheel, but it kept spinning around. Finally, he wedged himself between the side of the cage and the wheel and looked over Jovahn's shoulder.

But it was more than a code—it was Marks. The page

197

was a printout of the Midnight Academy Marks. Malcolm recognized the ones he knew: "Get out—fast!" "Safe here." Even some of the old ones like "dwell here," and the triangles, which turned out to mean "tell a good story." Some of the Shadow Signs were there too, like "this is the place." And ones he had never even seen before.

But how could this be? It was a strange-enough co-incidence that the Midnight Academy and the Striped Shadow used the same symbols, but that they were all on the Internet was, as Kiera would say, *freaky.*

Kiera read the top of the page: "'The Hobo Code. This code was a way that hoboes—homeless people who trav-eled—communicated to one another. They would leave this code on fence posts or street corners to warn or ad-vise other hoboes. It was most widely used in the 1930s, when many people were out of work and traveling around the country.' But why would Amelia send us this?" she asked. "Wouldn't it be more normal to send a message like 'Having a good time, but the fifth-graders here smell funny. Miss you.'"

You smiled, Mr. Binney. "Well, that doesn't really sound like Amelia's style. But as for why she sent it, I don't know." Just then, the phone rang. "What do you think?" you asked as you left to answer it.

Once you were out of earshot, the nutters burst into furious whispers. "Hoboes again!" Jovahn said. "First the coins, now this."

"But what do hobo men from the 1930s and a bunch of classroom pets today have in common?" wailed Kiera. "No offense, Jovahn. But this is nuts!"

"Well, maybe . . ." Jovahn started. Then he shook his head. "Naw, I got nothing."

He and Kiera turned to Skylar, who had been quiet this whole time. "What?" Skylar said. He was picking frosting off his shoelaces.

"Well, usually this is where you say something brilliant or point out the obvious," Kiera said grumpily.

Skylar stared at the page. "It's kind of cool," he offered. "I love codes. It's like a secret story or a message, in plain sight. You only see it, really, if you speak the language."

A secret story. Skylar was right. It *was* a secret story. That was exactly how the Midnight Academy used them. Messages in plain sight of lankies and nutters, but only readable to critters because they knew the language.

Malcolm watched them talk, a warm feeling growing in the empty, cut-out space in his chest. His nutters were close, but he had a piece of the puzzle they didn't: McKenna's letter. And with this email—which Malcolm Knew with a capital *K* was actually meant for him—Amelia cemented what Malcolm had concluded the night before: The hobo's blue jay *was* Blue, the bird in the library. And Malcolm would bet anything it was Blue who had bought the Hobo Code, learned in his travels with Ernie Bowman, the hobo man, to the Academy.

Wait a minute . . . Malcolm said that again in his head. Ernie Bowman, the hobo man. Bowman . . . ho*bo* man.

Malcolm remembered then a time when Tianna and Kiera had gotten so mad at each other over a misunderstanding. Kiera had said "turn," Tianna heard "earn" and then told Susan "worm," and the whole story had gotten out of whack. Malcolm remembered, too, Aggy telling them, so long ago, how the Academy records used to be passed on, critter to critter.

Well, what if that had happened in the Academy? What if, through the years of critters telling this story over and over again, "hobo man" became "Bowman"? Could that be why there wasn't an "Ernie Bowman" mentioned with the blue jay in the yearbook? Maybe the hobo *had* been the handyman . . . what was his name? Randall Carson. Malcolm's whiskers twanged. If he was right, that could mean the hobo man, with his suspenders, had become . . . the original Elastic Order of Suspenders?

And if all *that* was the really case, then there was still one part left: Where did the name "Ernie" come from?

CHAPTER 25
NOTICING

Malcolm waited nervously at the top of the stairwell near the auditorium's balcony entrance. It was four o'clock. A time he shouldn't be out of his cage. But that was the least of his worries.

Ms. Brumble rounded the corner with her cart. She paused at the bathroom, checking it for paper towels and toilet paper. She was almost to the steps where Malcolm was. Malcolm glanced up the stairs.

"What's going on?" a voice hissed from the darkness of the floor above. "Why did that owl tell the Striped Shadow to send me here?" Snip stepped out of the shadows on the landing.

It had taken all of Malcolm's skills and favors to get

Beert to fly a message to the Striped Shadow for him. When Malcolm had told him it was for Snip, Beert almost wouldn't do it; there are some things that are harder to forgive. But eventually, for Malcolm's sake, he agreed to pass it along to the Striped Shadow to give to Snip.

Malcolm ducked under the radiator. He reached a paw out to touch the fuzzy object he had brought up from the Dictionary Niche. Yes, he should do this. McKenna would.

Snip strolled about the landing. "Hiding already?" She sniffed. "School still smells the same."

Ms. Brumble moved her cart again, and the noise made Snip freeze. Her tail straightened out like a fuzzy drumstick. "Who's that?" She crouched so she was on the same level as Malcolm under the radiator. "What is going on?"

Malcolm nodded out at the hallway below. Ms. Brumble and her cart were in sight now. "I'm giving you what you *need*," Malcolm finally said. "That's Ms. Brumble."

"I know that." Snip swiveled her head to follow Malcolm's gaze. Her whiskers quivered as she sucked in a breath.

Malcolm whispered fast. "What I told you in the boiler room last fall was true. She is your nutter, all grown up. Veronica Brumble. The one who lost you."

"I know!" Snip said in a voice so low that it was almost a moan. "I already know all that. What was the other thing you said . . ." Her voice trailed and her tail twitched as Ms. Brumble banged her broom on the edge of the cart.

"The other part's true too," Malcolm said. "She didn't

mean to leave you that day. To lose you. She broke her
ankle, and in the confusion, you got left behind. It was just
a terrible, terrible accident . . . for both of you."

Malcolm reached back for it and opened his mouth to
say more—with dignity and decorum—but suddenly
three nutters burst into the hallway below. Snip flinched
and retreated to the dark corner of the stairwell.

"Ms. Brumble!" Jovahn called. "We've been waiting for
you all day!" Malcolm's nutters! What were they doing
here? After school?

"Well, not all day, obviously," Kiera said, a little out of
breath from her run down the hall. "But Mr. Binney said
—well . . . we are wondering if we could look upstairs?
We decided we're not giving up. After finding the time

capsule, we want to find that portrait of McKenna for the next listening session. And I know you looked up there, but we thought, well, the of us—"

"Slow down, Kiera!" Ms. Brumble laughed. "Geez, I work the night shift because I like the quiet. I'm not used to all this commotion. Now, what's going on?"

Kiera took a deep breath and smoothed her hair. "We are still looking for that portrait of Walton McKenna. The one Skylar knocked down. We were thinking in class that if we could find it, we could show it at the next school board meeting like Amelia wanted. And Mr. Binney said that if we asked nicely, you might take us up to the third and fourth floors to look for it?"

Ms. Brumble's mouth raised in a half smile. "Mr. Binney said that, did he?" She looked around. "I notice he's not here."

"He had a meeting with Skylar's Gram," Jovahn added. "She's giving us a ride home."

At his name, Skylar snapped to attention. Then he pointed up the stairs. "There's a cat."

What?! Oh, gristle! Malcolm darted. But he was hiding under the shadows of the radiator, so the people couldn't see *him*. Snip, however, was out in the open. In the shadowy corner but exposed, nonetheless. Malcolm sensed her stiffen. *Please don't freak out*, Malcolm thought. *Please don't freak out.*

"Um—what?" the other three said.

"A cat," Skylar said, pointing again. "Look. At the top of the stairs."

The group peered up the stairs into the darkness. "There *is* a cat," said Kiera, stepping up closer. "Here, kitty, kitty," she called.

Snip glanced wild-eyed at Malcolm under the radiator. She was cornered. And Malcolm's internal pleas changed from *Please don't freak out* to *Please don't hurt Kiera.*

"Kiera . . ." Ms. Brumble called. "Be careful. Come down. Let me take a look first. There shouldn't be a cat in here. She's probably a stray."

But Kiera was there now. On the landing. "It's okay," she called back. "I think she's scared. Aren't you, kitty?" Kiera held out her hand. It was inches from Snip's nose. Malcolm could hear Snip's ragged breathing.

PLEASE don't hurt Kiera.

Malcolm realized he was holding his breath. Snip sniffed Kiera's fingers, and Kiera lightly touched them onto Snip's head. "It's okay, kitty. We're here. We'll take care of you." Malcolm had never heard Kiera use this voice. It was not harsh-bossy or glitter-spangles. It was soft, like chocolate left in a pocket too long.

Kiera lightly stroked the top of Snip's head with her fingers. Snip closed her eyes and swayed. A small sound generated from deep in her chest. A low, vibrating noise. A purr. Snip jerked her eyes open, looking wildly around.

Kiera laughed. "It's okay, kitty. Come on." Kiera tapped

the floor in front of her, and to Malcolm's amazement (and Snip's too, from the look she kept shooting over her shoulder at Malcolm), Snip followed her to the top step. Kiera sat a few steps down from her, so they were on the same level. She ran her hand over Snip, starting at her ears all the way down to her tail.

Snip shuddered. And leaned into Kiera's hand. She purred again.

Ms. Brumble was there now, a few steps lower. She smiled. "She likes you." Ms. Brumble reached out her hand, and Snip sniffed it, too. "I used to have a kitten that looked a lot like this," Ms. Brumble said. "Years ago. She ran away."

Now, thought Malcolm. It had to be now.

He reached back under the radiator for the fuzzy pink stuffed mouse and kicked it as hard as he could toward Ms. Brumble. It bounced, then rolled. It came to a rest next to Snip on the top step. He was about to find out if his hunch was right.

Kiera picked up the mouse and looked behind her. "Where in the world did this come from?"

Both Ms. Brumble and Snip stared at it, eyes wide.

"I—That's a cat toy," Ms. Brumble said in a shaky voice. "Mr. Plumpkins," she whispered. She gaped at Snip. Then took a step back. "I have to sit down."

But Kiera was already swinging the toy by its tail in front of Snip. "Here you go, kitty." And Snip—whether it was because of the ancient catnip, or Kiera's voice, or because she finally had something she *needed*—raised a paw and swiped at it.

"If she's a stray, do you think I can keep her?" Kiera asked, scratching her behind the ears.

At Kiera's question, Ms. Brumble finally took her eyes off Snip. "Well, I don't know . . . I guess that would be up to your parents—be careful!"

Kiera had picked up Snip and was now carrying her down the stairs. "I'm going to ask them," Kiera declared. "If they let me dye my hair for the fifth grade musical, a cat as sweet as this one shouldn't be any problem."

Malcolm finally let out his breath as Snip descended the stairs in Kiera's arms. Snip looked back up at where Malcolm was, still hidden under the radiator. And for the first time since Malcolm had known her, he saw her relax. Saw her melt into Kiera's arms, into a ball of black fur with yellow eyes and a white-tipped tail. Over Kiera's shoulder, Snip's whiskers twitched at Malcolm, and—Malcolm's stomach flipped—what was that? A smirk? A grimace? A sneer? What was Snip up to?

Then Malcolm realized why he couldn't recognize it: It was the start of a smile.

Malcolm hadn't even known that was possible.

CHAPTER 26

BEHIND McKENNA

Now what? Malcolm wondered as he crept out from under the radiator to listen to the nutters and Ms. Brumble chattering in the hall below. Malcolm could hear their voices receding as they made their way down the hall. Jovahn was still trying to convince Ms. Brumble to go look for the portrait upstairs. She was saying they needed to call animal services for the cat. Kiera was insisting that her dad would take the cat to the vet. Skylar was trying not to trip on his shoelaces.

Malcolm watched them move away from the landing. So . . . he guessed that had worked? It hadn't gone as planned, but from the looks of things, Snip didn't seem to mind. He smiled to himself. It was a little like Aggy's kale and butternut squash. He had a feeling that Snip would like this kale much better than her old butternut squash of the fourth floor. He just hoped she also enjoyed lots of loud singing.

Then, suddenly: "Hey!" Kiera cried. Snip stiffened in her arms. The cat's ears perked up, and she twisted so that her yellow eyes lasered in on Malcolm at the top of the stairs.

Kiera and Snip struggled for a moment; then Snip leaped down and raced back down the hallway toward Malcolm. "Hey!" Kiera shouted again, and took off after Snip.

What the crumb? *Now* what was Snip up to? Ms. Brumble called out, "Wait! Kiera! Oh . . . for Pete's sake!" And *she* chased after Kiera. Jovahn and Skylar didn't even hesitate. And in seconds, the whole group was churning up the stairs, aiming right for Malcolm.

Scrap! Malcolm dove out of the way as Snip reached the landing. The cat rounded the corner and continued up the next flight of stairs. As she did, Malcolm thought he heard, "Come on, rat!"

Malcolm hesitated for a second, then zigged and zagged after the group, dodging Skylar's untied shoelaces, which slapped the floor like whips.

Snip led them on a weaving, roundabout chase up to her domain: the closed fourth floor. Through a jungle of old tables, broken chairs, and chalkboards that had long ago been replaced. Back to a corner that Malcolm didn't even know existed. Finally, she stopped. She wasn't even breathing hard. Her yellow eyes gleamed as she waited for the humans and Malcolm to catch up.

Malcolm, on the other hand, was wheezing. He had followed in the shadows, darting from one to another. It was too dangerous to run out in the open. He watched, panting, behind the legs of two tables stacked on top of each other.

Kiera had managed to gather Snip in her arms again. "Kiera, be careful!" Ms. Brumble chided. "Obviously, that cat is unpredictable. And you guys"—she aimed her broom, which was still in her hand, at the other nutters —"shouldn't be up here! You're going to get me fired! Now, let's go. I don't want to hear another word about not calling animal services."

But Skylar was pointing again. And Jovahn was already kneeling and not listening. Malcolm climbed up to the next level of stacked tables so he could peer down.

"Dude, it's the *dude*," Jovahn whispered.

Kiera pushed her way between Skylar and Jovahn. "Oh . . . kitty! You've done it!" She rubbed Snip's ear, and Snip stretched her neck into Kiera's. "You've found Walton McKenna."

Because propped against a row of dented, paint-chipped lockers, leaning amid a stack of old chalkboards, was a painting. A painting of a man in an old-fashioned suit, with gray hair and round wire-rimmed glasses. His right hand rested on the head of an enormous floppy-eared dog.

Skylar touched a tear in the canvas over Walton McKenna's left elbow. "That's where I hit it with my shoe." Then he turned and looked at Snip with round eyes. "Can you believe it? She heard us talk, and she brought us to it!"

There was a pause, and then Ms. Brumble said, "Oh, Skylar. That was just a coincidence." She knelt down to study the painting. "We just trapped her in this corner. Or

she was tired and stopped here." But Malcolm saw her stealing glances at Snip out of the corner of her eye.

The nutters were quiet behind her. She stood and looked around. "What? You don't think so?" Finally, she shrugged and smiled. "What do I know?"

Jovahn reached out and gently fist-bumped Snip's paw. "Way to go."

"I suppose . . . since we found it, we might as well bring it down," Ms. Brumble said. She handed her broom to Skylar. "Jovahn, can you grab the other side?" Together, they wound their way back through the fourth floor and down to Room 11.

They continued the debate over how the portrait was found all the way back to the room, where Skylar's Gram was waiting to give everyone a ride home. You had some raised eyebrows over the cat, Mr. Binney, but Kiera's parents were called and, like she predicted, she was picked up by her dad, who took them directly to a vet.

In fact, the debate over how the portrait was found became part of the story—part of the whole legend, really —from that day on. Did the cat lead them to the portrait, or was that just a coincidence?

What do you think, Mr. Binney?

No one asked Malcolm. But he knew.

He Knew.

CHAPTER 27

ERNIE BOWMAN

Later that night, Malcolm called in a Ripe Tomato Alert to Room 11. He could never remember all the Midnight Academy alerts and what exactly they meant, but he knew a Ripe Tomato would get everyone there. Fast.

Maybe too fast. Polly came winging in. Honey Bunny loped in with Tank's scooter in his teeth. He was moving so quickly, the scooter flung right past the door and banged into the wall. Tank slid off and landed on his back. "What is it, Malcolm?" Honey Bunny gasped.

"Uh . . ." Malcolm was quickly realizing that maybe he had made a mistake with the kind of alert he had called. He looked past Honey Bunny. "Are you all right, Tank?"

Jesse James and Billy the Kid were pushing him back over onto his feet.

Tank craned his neck around. "I think I chipped my shell."

Aggy came trudging up, her glasses on her nose, Pete clamped tightly to her ruff. "What's"—*gasp*—"wrong"—*gasp*—"Malcolm?"

"Uh . . ." Malcolm said again. He looked around the circle of the Academy. They looked prepared to do battle. "First let me just say I'm sorry to get you all in a panic. I didn't get the full pledge training, you know. It's *possible* that I made the wrong alert call."

Harriet looked around. "So there's no emergency? I left a brand-new library book and there's not an emergency?"

"Not exactly," Malcolm admitted, then rushed to add, "But that's not to say there isn't something very important to share."

Harriet grumped, "Perhaps you need to have a nutter read you the story of the boy who cried wolf."

"You mean 'the rat who cried Ripe Tomato'?" Jesse joked, and elbowed his sister.

"Okay, okay," Aggy said, pushing her way forward. "What's this about, Malcolm?"

Then she looked behind him. Her tongue flicked out. Once. Twice. "Is that . . . what I think it is?" she finally asked. Slowly, the group fell silent as they followed her gaze.

Malcolm nodded so hard, he swore he could feel his

brain rattle a little. "Yes, I'm sorry to get you all worried. But we found . . . well, the nutters . . . actually *Snip* . . . now, that's a really long story!" He laughed weakly. "We found the portrait of Walton McKenna. And . . ." He paused in a dramatic way that Kiera would definitely approve of. "Let me present Ernie himself."

Instead of the gasps of recognition and congratulatory slaps on the back like Malcolm's hero brain had prepped him for, his statement was greeted with a lot of confused sideways glances.

Finally, Billy spoke up. "I thought you just said it was Walton McKenna?"

"It is," said Harriet flatly. "I've seen his picture in the yearbooks."

"Are you saying that Walton McKenna is Ernie Bowman?" Honey Bunny asked, his brow furrowed in a question mark.

"No," said Malcolm, realizing they were focusing in on the wrong thing. "No, no. Not the lanky! The critter. Look at the dog! Doesn't he look familiar? That's the dog from the coin. *His* name is Ernie."

Aggy crept forward to peer at the portrait with her glasses perched on her nose. "It *is* the same dog. But how do you know his name?"

"Let me start at the beginning. Remember 'In times of need, look beneath the oak under the stars behind McKenna'? Well this is 'behind McKenna.'"

Malcolm disappeared behind the painting for a moment. It wiggled and the Academy critters could see through the hole in the portrait that Malcolm was removing something from the back of it. He came around the front again, pulling several pieces of drawing paper.

He spread them out in front of the group. There were three sketches. The first was of someone's feet, wearing brand-new boots, crisscrossed and propped up against a fence post, with a dog's head resting on them. The dog had a dreamy look to his eyes. It was the same dog as the one in the portrait. "Ernie" was written at the bottom.

The second was a blue jay with one leg bent crooked. The artist had caught him in midflight, but from the background, you could tell it was inside. "'Blue,'" Billy read at the bottom of that page.

And the third. This was of a little girl—her back to the viewer, but peeking over her shoulder. "'Thomas Jefferson, guinea pig extraordinaire,'" Tank read.

Harriet gasped. "Did you say 'Thomas Jefferson'? The guinea pig? As in, the founding member of our Midnight Academy?"

Malcolm nodded. They were finally getting it! By now, Malcolm was sweating all the way up to his ears. Is this how hard it is to teach every day, Mr. Binney? Malcolm wished he had your laser pointer and document camera to help explain. "Yes! That's Thomas Jefferson! I think Blue and Ernie were there at the beginning of the Academy too. Blue was the school mascot who lived in the library. She and Ernie were this guy's"—he pointed to the boots

—"pets. And he's Randall Carson. The guy who did these pictures. And *he's* the hobo man." Malcolm waggled his eyebrows. "Get it? Ho*bo* man?"

"You've lost me again, Malcolm," Honey Bunny said.

Malcolm pulled out McKenna's letter. "Just listen for a minute." And he read the letter. And he explained about Ernie Bowman being Ernie and the hobo man, and the commas, and even Amelia sending the copy of the Hobo Code from her new school.

"Cheez, Malcolm, were you going to keep any more secrets?" Jesse
asked.

"I wasn't keeping them secret!"
Malcolm said. "I just didn't put it
all together. Until now."

"So . . . the traveler is . . .
a hobo," Harriet started.
"And the dog—"
"Is Ernie."
Billy was start-
ing to bounce,
and Malcolm knew
that meant she got
it. "Ernie"—she
pointed to the dog
—"and the

hobo man. Founders of the Midnight Academy and the first member of the Elastic Order of Suspenders."

"Yes!" Malcolm let out a huge breath. Crumb, he should have told her first. She had explained it so much better — and in twenty words.

Honey Bunny cleared his throat. "I'm still back on Snip. She's *alive?*" He cocked his head at Malcolm. "And you didn't say?!"

"Later," Aggy murmured. She had been remarkably quiet throughout all of this. "So, if the time capsule is 'under the stars,' and this is 'behind McKenna,' we're still missing 'beneath the oak.'"

Malcolm could have kissed her. He hoped she knew that he had saved this for her. He flipped the pictures over and pushed them toward her. "I found a note on the back."

"'Look in the auditorium wall, under the oak, R.C.,'" she read. "And then a Mark." Four triangles — one large, three small. Malcolm had already used Amelia's Hobo Code to figure it out. "It means 'tell a good story,'" he explained.

"Cheez," Billy said. "That's a little more straightforward than our yearbook messages."

"I suppose he had a little more to work with," Honey Bunny pointed out. "Being able to hold a pencil and all."

"*Inside* — under the oak." Tank bonked his head on the wall lightly. "How'd we miss *that?* Duh — we're Inside critters, so probably it's going to be . . . Inside."

But Aggy wasn't listening to any of that. She was watch-

218

ing Malcolm. She nodded at the portrait. "You've already figured this all out. Did you already go down there and look? Is it there? The Loaded Stash?" she asked.

He shook his head. "I haven't gone. I've been waiting for you."

CHAPTER 28

TELL a GOOD STORY

Twenty minutes later, the group had reassembled—a little less hectically—in the auditorium. The giant fans were still running, so they had to shout, but the moon and starlight shone through the side windows—especially so now, without the Council Oak outside.

"I found it! Here!" Billy called out. And there, on the baseboard at the back of the auditorium, directly under Sylvia's former nest, was a Mark. Two circles almost touching.

"What is it?" Harriet asked, looking up at Aggy. "What does it mean?"

"It's another old one, not used anymore." She touched

it with a claw. "But definitely appropriate. It means 'never give up.'"

"This is it! The Loaded Stash," Pete crowed.

Jesse pointed to a vent on the wall—in fact, the very same vent had given Malcolm light so he could see that Sylvia was a squirrel the first time they met. "I bet we could get in there to see what's behind it." He elbowed Malcolm. "Let's go!"

But Malcolm was starting to get a funny feeling in his stomach. Kind of like when you fill up your tray in the lunch line, only to find out that you don't have any lunch money. "Um, guys," he began to say. Because he knew— *nothing* was behind that Mark in the wall. Why, how many times had he run past it in the last few weeks? Surely he would have seen something. This was going to be another dead end. Another disappointment.

But Honey Bunny and Aggy had already tugged the vent off the wall, and Jesse and Billy plunged in.

"Can you see anything?" Tank called.

"Well, it's dusty, and there are a lot of sticks—"

Malcolm ducked his head in. Those were probably the sticks he had knocked down from Sylvia's nest that first week. "You know—" he started.

"O-ho! And—*bingo!*" Billy interrupted. What followed was furious scrabbling. Finally, the two emerged, each with their oversize hamster cheeks bulging with—

"But those are just leaves!" Malcolm said. The same leaves he and Sylvia had used. "They're all over the bottom of that wall. I think they fell down when I rebuilt Sylvia's nest—"

He looked around. Every single last critter was snorting with laughter.

Jesse spit out his mouthful. "Leaves! You built Sylvia's nest out of this? Malcolm, these aren't leaves—it's *money!*"

"Money?" What? "But—I thought . . ." He closed his mouth. What he thought now was that he probably should stop talking before everyone choked from laughing so hard.

"Oh, Malcolm," Aggy said. "You do bring out the chuckles. I think we'd better add financial training to our new pledge handbook," she said to Octavius.

He saluted in agreement.

"There are at least several hundred dollars in there," Billy said. "I think we've found our Loaded Stash."

"Several *hundred* dollars?" Honey Bunny said with a frown. "Hmmm."

"What's wrong?" Malcolm asked. "That's a lot, right?"

"Yes, but . . . it's not going to be enough."

Aggy sighed. "He's right. It'll be exciting, but it's not going to save the school the way we hoped it would. The way *I* hoped it would."

Jesse and Billy went back in the wall to pull out the rest. Malcolm followed them. "So, all of this is money, huh?" He kicked at the "leaves."

"Yeah," Jesse said, smirking. "Too bad. You could have found this Stash the first time you were in here."

Billy was pulling out more bills. "Hey, there's another letter."

Another envelope, but it was too dark in the wall to see. The three friends pulled it out into the light. Pete snipped it open with his claw, and the critters gathered around to read.

It was short. And when they got to the bottom of it, Malcolm suddenly Knew what they needed to do to save the school. He hoped he could explain it right.

"The Loaded Stash is not the money," he said.

"Huh?" Polly said.

"This whole time," Malcolm continued, "we were look-ing for the Loaded Stash, thinking it was some treasure or pile of money that would save our school."

Jesse waved a pawful of bills at him, but Malcolm shook his head. "No, because don't you see? There's *never* enough money. I mean, yeah, maybe there's enough to fix this room up or rewire the building so the third-graders can print in the computer lab without the lights going out in the first grade room. But money runs out. What never runs out is *story*." He pointed his tail at the new letter. "We need to share this. Because that's what the Loaded Stash is: a story. Not a legend about treasure, but a story about a man—the man our school was named after—who did something unexpected, with huge results. Maybe it's enough to jolt the school board into doing something unexpected too.

"Some wise critter once told me, 'You have no idea how many times the lankies don't know exactly what they need to know until the Academy helps them to see it.' The humans think they need money to fix this school. But what they need is a story. The legend of Ernie and the hobo man. Let's give it to them."

Whew! Malcolm wasn't sure if he had ever, *ever* talked that much. Or if it had ever mattered more.

It was quiet for a minute, as everyone thought it through. Finally, Honey Bunny spoke up. "Well, as some wise critter once told *me:* What do we have to lose?"

"It might not work, Malcolm," Aggy said. "You should know that. Money is a funny thing to lankies. It matters more than we can ever understand."

Malcolm remembered Amelia's move. Ms. Brumble and your conversations about your upcoming wedding.

"I know," he admitted. "But we've got to try. We can give them this money, but let's give them the story, too."

Slowly, Aggy nodded her head, her ruff rustling. "This may be one of the most harebrained—no offense, HB— ideas I have ever heard. But I guess I expect no less from you, Malcolm." She turned to face the rest of the group. "Let's make the lankies see it. Let's use the legend of Ernie and the hobo man to keep our school open."

Then she turned back to Malcolm. "So . . . what exactly did you have in mind?"

CHAPTER 29

THE ELASTIC ORDER
OF SUSPENDERS

So here it is, Mr. Binney. We're to the point in the story where things got a little messy for you. The Academy (and the McKenna All-Stars, for that matter) would like to apologize for any confusion and uncomfortableness on your part. But there's this funny thing. The world doesn't listen to nutters and critters. Not like it should, anyway. Both of them get a lot of pats on the heads, but not true listening. The Academy has always known this. That's why they operate the way they do—with an Elastic Order of Suspenders. A lanky to be their voice. Randall Carson, the hobo man, was their first voice.

And that's what the Midnight Academy needed now. A reliable, credible lanky.

You.

And Ms. Brumble,[1] of course.

The *new* Elastic Order of Suspenders.

The next morning, Malcolm was exhausted but wired. He jogged on his exercise wheel. In part to stay awake, in part because of nervous anticipation. Would you see? Would you notice?

You came in early, as you usually did, Mr. Binney. Before the rest of the building had really started waking up. You were maybe not all the way woken up either, because it took you a ridiculously long time to notice anything. You sipped coffee. You ran copies. You put everyone's journals back on their desks. You readied the dry-erase board with the morning's math warm-up and vocabulary word of the day. Then finally you sat down.

You shuffled papers for a bit—do you remember, Mr. Binney?—and then your eyes locked on a small stack of photocopies. You picked them up. You scanned them. You frowned and flipped through them again.

And then you walked over to the portrait, which was still leaning against the bulletin board. Only now, there was a paper sticking out of Skylar's tear. A small corner. You were tugging at it, and were just about to flip the portrait over so you could get at it from the back of the frame,

---

[1] There have never been two members of the Elastic Order of Suspenders at the same time. But the Midnight Academy is also pretty sure there's never been a teacher engaged to a custodian at McKenna before, either. And they couldn't decide on which one of you. So, there you go.

when Mrs. Rivera came in, holding photocopied pages identical to yours.

Malcolm felt his whiskers quiver. The plan was in motion.

"Morning, Mark," Mrs. Rivera said, waving the papers. "I came in to the strangest pages on my desk this morning. An incredible story—telling me to look in the wall of the

auditorium. So I did. And you're not going to believe this, but—"

"There's money in the wall?" He waved his pages also. "I got them too."

"Where did they come from? I know someone found the time capsule the other day. Is the money from that?"

She stopped as she finally saw what you were doing. "Where did you get this portrait?"

"Um, Ronnie—Ms. Brumble—found it when she was cleaning last night. And I think this portrait is where the pages came from . . ." You succeeded in getting the back off the painting, and the drawings fell out and drifted to the floor.

Mrs. Rivera picked them up. "These are the originals," she said, and frowned. "But how did we get copies before the originals came out of the painting? What is going on in this school?"

You shook your head. "I . . . don't know." Did Malcolm imagine it, or did you quickly glance his way and back?

Mrs. Rivera folded the pages back up crisply. "Well, it's certainly interesting." She looked around at the aging room. "Wonder what other secrets this building holds."

"I was thinking," you started. "Maybe we should—"

"Maybe we should send this story to the press and the school board?" She smiled. "Oh, yes, I think so. About time someone heard something good that's been going on at McKenna."

Finally, Malcolm stopped jogging. He let his wheel spin

without him, and it slowly came to a stop. *Yes, what a good idea*, he thought. Such a good idea that Octavius had already done it, emailing the copies from a dormant email account to the local newspaper and television station.

Was Mrs. Rivera surprised when she returned to her office and there was already a message from the newspaper, asking her to call them back about the money found in the wall of the school?

CHAPTER 30

SOCKS

It turned out that Malcolm and the Midnight Academy were not the only ones cooking up a surprise. You had your own, didn't you, Mr. Binney? Probably Malcolm should have guessed it. The vocabulary word of the day on the dry-erase board was "reunion."[1] In retrospect, it also must have been hard to keep this surprise—it's been Malcolm's experience that the happy secrets are the hardest to keep.

Skylar stumbled in that morning with his usual commotion. "Sorry we're late," he announced, and proceeded

---

[1] Reunion = when people who have been separated for a period of time come together again. Example? Read on.

to drop his pile of books, notebooks, and folders in the doorway. Papers went flying everywhere.

You stood. "Yes, now, class. Today we have a surprise visitor—" But before you could finish, someone stepped into the doorway behind Skylar. She stooped to help him pick up his mess. Her black hair swung forward, hiding her face.

Jovahn cried out, "Amelia! But what are you doing here?" He raced over and picked up the notebooks, since both Skylar's and her hands were full of six months' worth of Skylar's comics.

At the sound of Amelia's name, Malcolm raised up on his hind legs, his heart galumping. Amelia? Yes, it was Amelia! Standing in the doorway, between Skylar and Jovahn, as if she had never left! But . . . how?

You grinned, Mr. Binney. "So, yes, class, the surprise visitor this morning is . . . Amelia. She's here to spend the day with us. Amelia, why don't you take your old seat? You and Skylar can share the table this morning."

"But—but—" Jovahn sputtered, trailing after Amelia and putting Skylar's books on the table. "You're moving back?" he said hopefully.

She shook her head. "No, I wish. I'm only visiting. Skylar's Gram met my parents at the school board hearing. She felt bad how things ended. She says we need to finish what we started—the presentation for the school board. So, here I am."

Skylar jumped in. "My Gram didn't mind picking her up at her new apartment. She has to drive me anyway ever since I accidentally let all those crickets go on the bus last week. And she says . . ." He smiled shyly. "She says it's good to support your friends."

Amelia looked down at her feet at that. And wiggled her toes. "I guess I was so excited to come back, I forgot my shoes!" She looked up with a huge grin, huger than anything Malcolm had ever seen. Huger than the moon next to the stars Outside.

The rest of the class laughed with her. Kiera stood up then. "Don't worry. I have some in my locker you can borrow. They're pink ballet flats with sparkles on the toes. They'll be super cute with those green socks. Can I get them, Mr. Binney?"

You nodded and pointed at Malcolm. "And while she gets them, you'd better say hello to someone before he passes out, Amelia."

Sure enough, Malcolm was racing around in his cage. His tail-safe exercise wheel couldn't contain his energy, so he ran laps. Around and around his cage. He was moving so fast that on the short ends, he ran up on the walls. And every time he passed Amelia, sitting in her place where she belonged, he tossed shredded paper up in the air. Amelia was here.

Amelia was here!

The McKenna All-Stars got permission to meet in the library for afternoon recess. You stopped by for a few minutes, Mr. Binney, to drop off some cupcakes and fill everyone in on the morning's developments with the portrait.

"And I have a cat now!" Kiera was explaining. "We found her upstairs. I call her Blackberry. Ms. Brumble gave me the idea for the name."

Amelia jerked her eyes wide in Malcolm's direction. "What?"

Subtly, Malcolm underlined the word "later" on Amelia's notebook with his tail.

"But where did you find that Hobo Code?" Jovahn said. He was leaning over Amelia, *still* not eating his cupcake. Malcolm worried something might be permanently wrong with him. Who could ignore a cupcake?

"I was searching about hobo coins online. And that led me to hoboes, which led me to the Hobo Code. And as soon as I saw it, I knew it was connected somehow. Because Malcolm showed me the Marks." She turned to the group. "So, what's the All-Star plan now?"

"We still thought we'd present at the last board meeting," Kiera started. "What we had before, only show the time capsule and the portrait now. It'd be even better if you could come too."

What? Malcolm sat up. The same presentation? After all this? No, no, no. Malcolm had to show them. But how to explain? It would take forever with his notebook. He needed something faster, something shorter. Something straight to the point.

Like a Mark. Or two.

Malcolm stuck his tail in Jovahn's cupcake frosting.

"Hey!" Jovahn protested. (Well, if he wasn't going to eat it . . .)

With his tail dipped in blue, Malcolm drew two circles on Jovahn's napkin. Two circles close together, then beneath them, a large triangle followed by three small ones.

Amelia peered at them. Then she pulled a paper out of her back pocket. She smoothed out her copy of the Hobo Code.

"'Never give up,'" Skylar said, deciphering the circles.

"And 'tell a good story,'" Kiera added.

"You know, a story does always make things more interesting," Jovahn said. "That and adding bathroom jokes. Do you think . . ."

"No," said Kiera emphatically. "Do *not* tell that bathroom joke of yours again."

"I agree," Amelia said. "But Mr. Binney did give us a pretty good story to tell." The All-Stars looked at one another, then at Malcolm.

"So it's decided," Kiera said with a laugh. "We'll mix up our presentation a little bit tomorrow night. It can't go worse than the last time!"

Amelia licked frosting off her fingers then and stood. "You know, speaking of stories—I want to see that Niche behind the dictionary again." She smiled and tilted her head. "Anyone want to take a look with me?"

"Amelia!" Jovahn glanced at Mrs. Snyder, who was leaning over a group of fourth-graders in the computer lab next door. "Someone will see!"

Amelia laughed and stretched her arms wide. "What are they going to do? I don't go to this school anymore. One of the few perks about something bad happening to

you is that you realize you don't need to worry so much about the little stuff. But if it'll make you feel better"—she scooped Malcolm up into her hoodie—"Malcolm will keep watch," she said. Then she walked over to the dictionary shelf and carefully stacked the books as she pulled them off it. The other nutters gathered behind her.

"Wow, you can hardly even notice that," Jovahn whispered as Amelia felt for the handle on the hidden cabinet door. It popped open with a little squeak. Skylar lay down on his belly to peer in. The others crouched around. Malcolm wondered if Mrs. Snyder would notice Skylar on the floor, but then he reconsidered: Skylar sprawled out was maybe not that unusual.

"Whoa!" Skylar said. "You should see all the junk in here! This is worse than my desk!"

Amelia reached past him. She pulled out a blue feather. "Look," she said, holding it up. "Do you think . . . ?"

Kiera laughed. "It *is* like your desk, Skylar. There's even a stash of comics."

Skylar stuck his arm in and pulled out the pile of comics and magazines. He flipped through them. Almost immediately, he jumped to his feet. He crashed into a table. "Oh my gosh," he said, shoving the whole pile at Kiera. "Keep me away from those!" he said.

The other nutters stared at him.

"I'm serious!" he shouted, causing Mrs. Snyder to peer in from the computer lab. "We show Mr. Binney this.

237

With—" He grabbed a sticky note off the library counter and jotted down a phone number. "With this number. But until then—they've got to stay safe in there. Promise me." He grabbed Jovahn's collar with both hands and shook him. "And no matter what, do NOT let me touch them."

CHAPTER 31

THE VOTE

Two weeks later, Malcolm made his way to the library. The rest of the Academy was already gathered around the computer. The final listening session—at the school board office this time, because McKenna's auditorium was still unusable—was about to begin. Because this meeting was so important to McKenna, though, the district Midnight Academy had rigged up a web camera in the ceiling of the board office so the McKenna Academy could watch live.

Malcolm felt like it was his first day at McKenna all over again—stomach: nervous-jumpy; feet: sweaty; whiskers: nibbled down to nubs.

The board members sat in a half circle at a U-shaped

table in the front of the room. A podium was set up to the right of them, so speakers could be seen by both the board and the audience. And the audience? It was last-day-of-school-carnival crazy. Seriously, Malcolm didn't think another nutter or lanky could fit in the room. Not even the baby size. At the far back, television cameras filmed. The whole room buzzed, more than nutters, even, in the moments right before the bell rang to start winter break.

The mustached man from the first meeting rapped a small wooden hammer on the table. "Welcome, everyone. It's great to see such a nice turnout for this last hearing about McKenna Elementary School. We will be voting on our decision following comments from the public tonight. As you all are aware, some . . . events have come up since our last meeting, but before we address those, we'd like to finish the first meeting. The last time we were together, there was a group of fifth-graders from McKenna who were presenting their opinions when . . . well, we all know how that meeting ended. We'll hear from them first, then take comments from the rest of you. The sign-up sheet to speak is . . ." There was a small commotion from the board around him. "Oh! I guess the sign-up sheet is full for tonight!" A small smile rippled through his mustache. "So let's begin."

Then, there she was—Malcolm's Amelia—standing between Kiera and Jovahn, and wearing her favorite green hooded sweatshirt over a blue dress and black tights. The sweatshirt didn't match at all, and Malcolm Knew that it was worn for him. He had spent so many wonderful hours in that hood! Honey Bunny nudged Malcolm and wiggled his pink nose at him. "You okay, Malcolm?" he whispered.

Malcolm nodded.

Kiera stepped to the microphone. "Our teacher, Mr. Mark Binney at McKenna Elementary School, always says that a school is more than a building. We think so too. But we're not here tonight to simply tell you why you should keep our school open. We're here tonight to tell you a story." Jovahn and Skylar pulled out the portrait of Walton McKenna. "If you've been watching the news at all the last few weeks, you probably know this man. And what he did with his money. He's Walton McKenna. A generous man who donated money to build many things in our community, including an addition to our school in the 1930s."

And she went on, telling about the time capsule and reading McKenna's letter and how he had helped the hobo man. She told about how that man—Randall Carson—had stayed on in Clearwater, working as a handyman at the new high school. How he continued to make art his whole life—including, even, this portrait of Walton McKenna and his dog, Ernie.

Kiera didn't go into the Midnight Academy's role, and the story really wasn't all that different from what had been in the news lately. But that's the power of telling a good story, Malcolm had learned. It never hurts to repeat it—because you don't know when people are really, truly listening.

"You've probably heard, too, that there was money found in the walls of our auditorium," Kiera finished up. "Not from Walton McKenna, like you might expect, but from Randall Carson. It wasn't a lot—seven hundred dollars. Mrs. Rivera, our principal, says that'll help us get a few new desks for next year. But it was a lot for Randall Carson. And more important, he left a note with that money. I'd like to end by reading it to you now."

She cleared her throat and took hold of the microphone. With a gulp of panic, Malcolm thought she might belt out "Rocky Top." But instead, she read out in a clear voice.

January 17, 1952

To whoever finds this money:

Our Clearwater community lost Mr. Walton McKenna today. You can look him up and see all the good things he's done, but I guarantee they won't all be listed there. You see, once, a long time ago, he gave me money I needed when I didn't deserve it. It made all the difference in my life.

In honor of this man, I've taken that money he originally gave me (plus a little gift of my own) and tucked it in this Mason jar. I feel sure that he would be tickled at the thought of it being discovered sometime in the future —hopefully, in someone else's time of need.

For you see, sometimes it is not the grand things you do
in life, but the small ones that make the biggest difference.
Mr. Randall Carson
Former traveler of the road
Current McKenna High School handyman

Malcolm pictured the note in his head. What Kiera
hadn't shared was the Mark drawn at the bottom. Two
circles next to each other: "Never give up."

After Kiera spoke, others came forward to tell a story
about McKenna Elementary School. Students. Former students. Teachers. Former teachers. Even Ms. Brumble spoke
about visiting with her kitten when her mom was working
as a principal.

Finally, they came to the end. Not one person had spoken about money or budgets or repairs or busing.

The members of the school board looked at one another.
Finally, a red-haired lady shook her head. She turned on
her microphone and spoke. "We hear you, we really do,"
she said to the crowd. "But money's money. And we don't
have it. Are we willing to keep this aging school open if it
means cutting a middle school music class? Or dropping
the all-school track-and-field meet for the fifth-graders in
May? Is keeping one school open more important than
these things? Couldn't this . . . this sense of community oc-
cur in the other buildings? Doesn't it? I'll bet we could have

representatives from Fairfax and Parkview here, and they could tell us stories just as wonderful. Maybe not quite as amazing as a lost fortune, but still. Wouldn't our students also find a home and community in those schools?"

Suddenly, Malcolm's insides twisted. Because she was right. For as much as he loved McKenna, did he love it at the expense of and cost to other schools and other nutters? Surely, the other students felt the same about their schools too. Had he been wrong in being so one-sided in his view? Was it like how he had seen Snip? So evil that he couldn't even believe that she had wants and needs and hurts that caused her to be who she was?

Malcolm lowered his head on his paws. Why couldn't things be more straightforward? Why wasn't right always right and wrong always wrong? It didn't seem fair. After all that Malcolm had done, maybe saving the school wasn't even really the right thing to do.

The meeting dragged on. Finally, the mustached man stood. "I'd like to say one more thing. And then it's time to call for a vote."

He looked out over the crowd for a moment. He even stared for a second directly into the Midnight Academy web camera and slid a thumb under his green suspenders. The McKenna Midnight Academy gasped.

"Do you think . . ." started Pete.

"He couldn't be—" Harriet said.

"Shhh!" Polly flapped. "He's speaking!"

"I'd like to propose a third option," the man said. "Perhaps we need more time. More time for this community support to show itself in a financial way. I move we add a third choice to the agenda tonight: keeping McKenna open for one more year, while we explore financing options. And then next year, we revote. I believe the district reserves can fund this for one more year." His eyes glinted as he raised his white eyebrows. "Perhaps after all these stories tonight, we have another Walton McKenna or Randall Carson in our midst."

"I second the motion," said a woman quickly at the end of the school board table.

The red-haired woman frowned. "I still say . . ."

The mustached man nodded. "We know. You've got very good points. But how about we vote on it?"

The secretary at the head of the table read the first choice. "Those who vote to keep the school open indefinitely." The table was silent. She paused and wrote something down. "Okay, and the new proposal: To keep McKenna open for the next school year, using district financial reserves. With a revote on this date next spring." The lights next to the school board microphones lit up green. Every single one, save one. The red-haired lady's. Finally, she said, "Oh, *okay.*" And pressed her button too.

Both the board room and McKenna's library erupted, but in a much different way than the last time. There was no water, no power outage, no critters running through the crowd. Just celebration. No one in the board room could even hear the secretary read the final choice. It was unanimous. McKenna would be open. For another school year, at least.

CHAPTER 32

OUTSIDE AND INSIDE

The Midnight Academy hooted and hollered. Jesse and Billy pulled out a bag of corn chips and baby carrots to celebrate. "We've been saving these for a special occasion. Hoping it was tonight!"

Pete danced with Aggy. Harriet got up on the table and did a funny little jig she called the hokey pokey. Polly swooped about the room in crazy circles. Tank pulled his head and legs in his shell and gave rides on his back to Billy and Jesse as Honey Bunny spun them around. Oscar did flip turns in his aquarium.

Malcolm took a turn on Tank's back and was flung off near the window. When the dizziness subsided, he realized that there was a face outside it, looking in.

Acer. Or the Striped Shadow. What was he doing here? Malcolm ran down the row of windows. The last one was still open.[1] "Acer?" Malcolm called.

"Hey, Malcolm," he said, as Malcolm climbed out onto the sill. "Just watching your party. Sounds like you got everything you wanted."

"Yeah," Malcolm said. "Yeah, we did. Even what we needed."

"So your nutters won't leave now?"

"The current ones will still move up, but there will be different ones next year. Aggy says that's the way it works. My nutters will move up to the middle school, and Pete's fourth-graders will be my fifth-graders next year."

"And what about your nutter—Amelia?"

"She came back to visit," Malcolm said quietly. "We got to say goodbye. And it's not all-the-way goodbye. I'm going to visit her new apartment on the weekends. And I'll be there for the summer. Mr. Binney will be busy with his wedding, so Amelia's going to take me."

"And you're okay with that?"

Malcolm shrugged. "I guess I have to be. It's not going to change it if I'm not. And maybe it'll be great. As a good friend put it, I have to be open to the possibilities of kale. I mean, I want my nutters to grow up. They can't stay fifth-graders forever. And liking kale doesn't mean I don't still love butternut squash."

---

[1] Unfortunately, Mrs. Snyder had been unable to close it ever since Michael had opened it to see the cat weeks earlier.

"Huh?" Acer tilted his head.

Malcolm smiled. "Never mind. It makes sense to me."

"Well, anyway, I was stopping by to say thank you for what you did for Snip. I saw her leave with that girl the other day—the sparkly one. She looked very content. I think you saved her, Malcolm."

Saved her. Huh. Funny how saving someone—you'd think it would be big and heroic, like the superheroes in Skylar's comics, but really, when it came down to it, Randall Carson was right. Saving someone could be done with something quite small. You just needed to pay attention. To notice, as McKenna put it.

Malcolm nodded, filing that away in his hero brain for next time. "Hey," he said. "What about Sylvia? Is she okay? Her squirrelings?"

The Striped Shadow gestured with his good front paw. "Oh, I found them a new place in a maple across the way. She got it acorn-cheap, if you know what I mean. I'm sure you'll see them around. Those little ones are still asking about something called corn dogs."

Malcolm's stomach rumbled, reminding him of the party behind them. "You want to come in and help us celebrate? There's all sorts of food."

"Naw. You know . . ."

"I know," Malcolm said, with a fake groan. "Outside and Inside critters don't mix."

Acer laughed. "Yeah." Then he grew serious. "Except when they do." He stuck his left front paw out and shook

Malcolm's. "And I'm glad we did. It's been a delight working with you, Malcolm. Your Inside critters—the two-legged ones, too—are lucky to have you."

Malcolm stood up straight. "Thanks," he said, trying to fill his voice with Midnight Academy–appropriate dignity and decorum. "And don't worry, your secret's safe with me."

Acer snorted. "Yeah, whatever that puffy-chest act is, it's still not working for you, Malcolm."

"Okay, then." Malcolm snapped Acer with his tail. "How's this: I won't even tell anyone what a big softy you *really* are."

Acer laughed again and slipped back into the darkness. He called over his shoulder in his deep Striped Shadow whisper: "You'd better not! The Shadow knows. The Shadow always knows . . ."

Malcolm shook his head and smiled.

Then he went back through the open window and joined in the Academy's festivities. He couldn't always know what was going to happen. No one could. But he couldn't—wouldn't—let that stop him from enjoying all this delicious kale around him.

There was a splash, and Malcolm was suddenly drenched. "Hey!"

Oscar had flipped something out of the aquarium. The first hobo coin, with Ernie on it. How had Oscar gotten it? Malcolm touched the dog's face. Saw up close the scratches that the hobo man had made so many years ago to carve Ernie into the nickel.

"Good work, Ernie and the hobo man," Malcolm whispered. He looked up at the critters dancing around the library. "Blue and Thomas Jefferson, too. You started something good here."

Dear Readers,

As sometimes happens with even the best of stories, they don't always end at the end. This one kept going, even after the writers (McKenna All-Stars, indeed!) finished writing it.

Because it turns out, not only do commas matter, but comics matter too.

Enjoy,

Mr. Mark Binney
5th Grade Teacher
Honorary Member of the
    Elastic Order of Suspenders

On a warm day at the end of May, the PA system suddenly squawked alive. "Good morning, boys and girls," Mrs. Rivera's voice greeted everyone. "I'd like to invite you to an all-school assembly in the semi-refurbished auditorium at nine o'clock. Teachers, please line up your classes and have them sit in their assigned seats promptly. See you then."

Room 11 burbled. As you know, Mr. Binney, at this point in the school year, fifth-graders long to be done with fifth grade, so anything to get out of the classroom was welcome. Kiera asked, "What's it about, Mr. Binney?"

You shrugged. "How about we go down to the assembly and see?" But you also hummed as you took atten-dance.

Jovahn poked Skylar, who was watching a family of squirrels play in the trees. "What do you think it is?"

"What?" Skylar said. "Oh, you mean the assembly? I don't know, but my Gram gave Amelia a ride to McKenna again this morning. She's waiting in the auditorium for us. She said Mr. Binney called her at home last night."

What?! Both Jovahn and Malcolm sat up like they had been zapped with one of Michael's hand buzzers. "This would have been good to know," Jovahn whispered at Skylar as the class lined up.

"Sorry," said Skylar, craning his neck toward the win-dow. "Do you think that's a mom and her babies? I won-der what baby squirrels are called?"

Jovahn shook his head, catching Kiera's attention. She asked, "Do you think this is . . . *you know?*" Only Kiera could get away with asking a question like that and expect anyone to understand it.

"No idea," Jovahn said, and Malcolm wondered if he was answering her question or commenting on her state-ment.

On their way out the door, you stopped Jovahn. "I think there's someone else who should be at this assem-bly." You nodded at the back of the room, where Malcolm was watching with his paws up on the wire of his cage. You pressed a small travel cage into Jovahn's hand. "Hang on to him. This is going to be a busy assembly. And we can't have him running around again."

When the class entered the auditorium, the room was already full of people milling about: kids finding their seats, teachers shushing them, and Mrs. Rivera waiting near the front of the room, chatting with several other adults. Skylar was right—Amelia was there too. Skylar's Gram had also stayed for the assembly. They filed in, past the newly repaired portrait at the back of the hall. Next to it were the hobo's drawings, each framed as well.

"Did Mr. Binney say anything?" Jovahn asked Amelia.

"No, he just asked if I could miss one more day of school."

"Well, Mr. Binney sure seems happy," Jovahn pointed out. And, in fact, you did. You were already in a seat next to Ms. Brumble, and—you were *holding hands*. In public. Something was definitely up.

Amelia raised her eyebrows. "What's Ms. Brumble doing here? She works nights." She took the cage from Jovahn.

"What are *you* doing here? You go to another school," Kiera pointed out.

In fact, there were a lot of people in the room who didn't necessarily belong. The school board. Retired teachers. The local news crew that had filmed the last school board meeting. And an elderly lady sat in the front, next to a guy in a ponytail and slouchy jeans.

Finally, the room settled down, and Mrs. Rivera walked

to the podium on the stage. The cameras were aimed in her direction. "Thank you all for coming," she said. "Welcome back to our auditorium. It's not quite put together yet, but it seemed important that we meet here. As you know, it's been an exciting year at McKenna. First we're closed, then we're not. Well, we're not quite done yet."

Kids looked nervously around and Mrs. Rivera laughed. "I apologize. I said that poorly. I'd like to assure you all that our school will be open again next year. But there's something more." She cleared her throat and continued: "Back in March, we opened a time capsule from 1938, when this very room was built. I think we were all hoping for treasure. Something to save our school. And we found it, but not in money or riches. In a story that reminded us all about what's really important."

She pulled out something in a plastic sleeve, and Jovahn kicked Amelia, who tightened her grip on Malcolm's cage. Malcolm let out a little squeak.

"Hey, that's—" started Skylar before Kiera shushed him.

"We've found a lot of things in strange places this year. And sometimes, in our rush to figure out how to save our school, we didn't notice them right away. One was this comic book. According to the note shared with the school board, I like to think it's part of that larger story I just mentioned. When Mr. McKenna gave his money to the man who was trying to steal it from him, he said that man bought a boy a comic book. We'll never know who that boy was. Or what he did with his comic. But I like to think that he stashed it in our school—and it has been waiting for us all these years."

She turned suddenly and gestured to the front row of the audience. "I'd like to invite up here Shirley Anne Vale, Mr. Walton McKenna's granddaughter." The room clapped politely as the elderly lady rose and walked slowly up the stairs to the stage.

"And Mr. Loomis, the owner of Quick Street Comics and Games." The man with the ponytail took the steps two at a time.

"Hey, that's Al!" some kid in the audience said.

"And finally, Skylar Morgan, from Mr. Binney's fifth grade class." The room of kids swiveled in their seats. Skylar froze until Jovahn literally pushed him down the aisle. The students in the audience rumbled. Skylar looked back, but Amelia and Jovahn waved him on. "He could at least close his mouth," Kiera said with a smile.

Finally, Skylar made it to the stage. "It was Skylar here who first noticed the comic," Mrs. Rivera said, placing her hand on his shoulder. "It's been my experience that every student has a Knack. Sometimes it takes a while for us to discover it. One of Skylar's many Knacks is noticing things that others might not. And that, along with his extensive comic book knowledge, led him to realize that we did, in fact, have a treasure in our midst. Mr. Loomis, perhaps you could explain?"

Al Loomis slicked his hair back to his ponytail and took the microphone. "Yeah. Um. That's not just any comic. That's a Superman comic. And it's not just any Superman comic, it's the *first* Superman comic. 1938." The kids in the room were silent, still not understanding. But the adults— the teachers, the media—started buzzing. Al continued, "This issue is incredibly rare. And collectible. This one's a little marked up, but the last first-edition *Superman* comic that was found in a quality similar to this one"—he held it reverently—"sold at auction for nearly a million dollars."

Now the room exploded. Nutters hooted and hollered. Mr. Binney and Ms. Brumble hugged—in front of everyone. Jovahn stood and let out a whistle so ear-piercing that Amelia elbowed him and pointed at Malcolm's cage. "Sorry, mousie!" Jovahn said, grinning.

Mrs. Rivera tried to get everyone's attention. "Our school district foundation will handle the proceeds, but this discovery will do a world of good. We've set up a scholarship fund. With it, we'll . . ." Her voice faded out as she realized no one was listening to her. Finally, she shrugged and flipped off the microphone. Grinning, she put her arm around Skylar.

Amelia stood up so Malcolm could see the room through his travel cage. And Malcolm stood on his hind legs to take it all in. His nutters. His school. His home. And even though his nutters would move on, he still had a summer with Amelia. And a new crop of nutters next fall

—there was always a nutter who needed a friend, Aggy said. And there was you, Mr. Binney. And, of course, the Midnight Academy.

Way up on the darkened balcony, in the shadows, a flash of white caught Malcolm's eye. He squinted. Was that the white tip of a cat tail? Snip—or rather, Blackberry— should be home at Kiera's. Malcolm couldn't quite make out who—or what—it was. But he hoped it was her.

After all, this was her school too.